BABOON

BABOON

Naja Marie Aidt
Translated by Denise Newman

Two Lines Press

Bavian © 2006 by Naja Marie Aidt & Gyldendal, Copenhagen.
Published by agreement with the Gyldendal Group Agency.
Translation © 2014 by Denise Newman

Published by Two Lines Press
582 Market Street, Suite 700, San Francisco, CA 94104
www.twolinespress.com

ISBN 978-1-931883-38-2

Library of Congress Control Number: 2014934782

Design by Ragina Johnson
Cover design by Gabriele Wilson

Printed in the United States of America

This project is supported in part by awards from the National Endowment for the
Arts and the Danish Arts Foundation.

ART WORKS.
arts.gov

THE DANISH ARTS FOUNDATION

Quotes in "The Honeymoon" from *William Blake: The Complete Poems.*
Edited by Alicia Ostriker. London: Penguin Books, 1977.

Contents

BULBJERG

Suddenly we found ourselves in the middle of an astonishing landscape: luminous, white sand dunes on all sides, wind swept, small trees twisting under the vast open sky. We gasped joyfully as though coming up for air after being under water too long. We stood there looking around, our eyes blinking after staring at the gravel road in the dark forest for so long. Even the smell was different here, salty and fresh, the sea had to be close by. But we lost our bearings long ago. We were going in circles. It was hot. We had a six-year-old boy and dachshund with us. The bikes were old and rusty, the danger of getting a flat was imminent. We stood completely still and listened. The wind moved through the leaves with a faint rustling, the birds sang, and then one shrieked, hoarse and desperate, as if for its life. Sebastian looked nervously at me. "It's just a buzzard. Nothing to be afraid of."

"Come here, Seba. Do you want a cookie?" You called the boy over with excessive gentleness, and I caught myself jerking my head around with an exaggerated and timid movement to look behind us. There was the forest we had come from, dark and still as a deep lake. The path stretched before us through what looked like a little birch grove, and beyond that the dense pine forest, moss, heather, and fallen trunks, grayish black with cracked branches sticking out like spikes.

"My legs are tired," complained Sebastian. Then he broke down—his dirty hands hid his face, his shoulders shook.

You took him on your lap.

Sitting in the grass, you rocked him back and forth while he cried. You looked at me with large worried eyes. I stared back. "What?" I said. "Nothing," you answered, stroking the boy's head. "It's going to be dark in four or five hours."

"So? What do you want me to do?"

You sighed.

I lay down with my arms under my head.

Sebastian is turning seven in fourteen days. In August, he will enter the first grade. In a way, he's the same as when he was a baby. The same slightly worried look, those little knit brows. It looks like he'll have an overbite. Then we'll have to go through all that with braces and headgear. I open my eyes and you are standing over me with a look of hatred. Maybe you've been standing there for a few minutes. "Shouldn't we get going?" you ask. I get up and suddenly notice how tired I am. My arms are completely limp and there's an overwhelming feeling of weakness throughout my entire body. The water bottle is empty. The dog pants with its tongue hanging out of its mouth. You lift it up into the cardboard box on the bike rack. Sebastian bravely picks up his bike and rides ahead of us. His bell rings with every bump in the road, and the flag he was so proud of when I mounted it on the rear mudguard looks cheap and shabby now. We ride on in silence. Every time we come to an intersection, you look inquiringly at me, but I'm not the local here, and so each time you end up saying something to the effect of: "So, um, I think we turn right here. I think

I remember that woodpile." Then, without a word, we turn right, until Sebastian throws himself on the ground, yelling and screaming. He's completely hysterical. He thrashes at us every time we get close. I use sour and you, sweet. In the end, I shake him hard, shouting that he should calm down or else we'll ride off without him, and then he can cry all he wants, until that buzzard comes and gets him. I regret the moment immediately and put him down. He bawls, holding onto my leg. You're sitting, leaning against a tree stump. Some ants are crawling up Sebastian's neck, dangerously close to his mouth. "What the hell?" I shout. He shrieks and throws himself to the ground. He spits and sputters and slaps himself in the face. I have to pull off all his clothes to brush off the ants. He flails and kicks. He's bit in several places. The snot runs from his nose. I pick up the naked boy and stand holding him for a while. He just whimpers now, pressing his face against my chest.

"If we're not riding in circles, we should reach Bulbjerg at some fucking point. It's impossible to ride in circles here, for Christ's sake," I say. "It's impossible in a shitty little forest like this," I hiss. "Anne!" I shout. You finally stand up, your face gray and streaked. You rub your eyes like a child. "I know the guy who owns the hotdog stand," you then say.

"What hotdog stand?" I ask irritated. "The stand near Bulbjerg," you whisper.

Sebastian breathes so close to my ear that it tickles terribly; I let him slide down to the ground. He wraps his arms around my hips.

"Seba, sit on the back of my bike," I say loud and furious.

I pull myself away from the child and fling the yellow kid's bike into the bushes. I think how it looks like evidence from a grisly crime. Someone will come across it one day. They'll find my fingerprints on the frame and Sebastian's on the handlebars. Perhaps yours as well. Maybe they'll think we murdered the child. "We'll get your bike another day," I assure Sebastian. He's sitting behind me, arms around my back, still naked, his legs dangling, and the fear that he'll get a foot caught in the wheel irritates me, the same way a mosquito waiting in the dark until you're about to fall asleep irritates.

We ride like this for nearly an hour; it's muggy, and I guess that it's almost six o'clock, but neither of us has a watch on. We left home at nine in the morning. It was supposed to be about ten miles from the summerhouse to Bulbjerg. We had wanted to see the beautiful ice-age landscape. I also wanted to show Sebastian the German bunker. We were going to have a good talk about the time of the Occupation.

When I woke up this morning, you were watching me. We were both lying on our sides, facing each other, and you were watching me. You smiled. The light fell from the skylight in a sharp diagonal line onto the white duvet. I felt like I was being spied on. Then Sebastian was standing in the doorway. He said the dog had peed on the rug in the living room. A little while later I could hear you laughing and chatting in the kitchen. We used to do it on that rug. We were here in the fall, it was cold, and in the evenings we lit the fire. I slowly peeled the clothes off her, and she looked beautiful on the red Persian rug, in the warm light from the fire. She spread her legs. She looked at me with dark, almost sorrowful eyes. Your sister has a tighter cunt than you. I wonder whether you're born that way, or if it's just because she's so young. Tine is only your half sister. Sebastian is adopted.

"No one in this goddamn family is really related," your stepfather always proclaims on Christmas and Easter when he gets up to make a toast. "Assholes!" he yells later, collapsing in his drunkenness, so that your cousins have to carry him out.

Now it's usually on the rug at home that I make love to her. That she makes love to me. When you're out and Tine babysits Sebastian. When he's sleeping. I enjoy looking at her when she's lying there, vulnerable and exposed on the cold floor, and at the same time protected by the carpet's soft pile. She's a little cold. She gives good head. Her palate is warm and hard, and she concentrates, always making it into a little performance. I miss her. I miss her thick brown hair, her warm neck, her profile when she's lost in thought with one hand under her chin, unaware that I'm standing there in the dim light watching her. I feel horny and desperate. It's come this far. I thought I could easily handle a couple of weeks' vacation up here; after all, we do have a child together.

We're riding down the hill at a good speed, and how it actually happens I have no clear recollection, but a stick gets caught in your spokes and I ram into your back wheel, the bikes flip, and the boy and the dog are thrown to the side: they both land in the ditch; Sebastian hits his head against a large rock and the sound it makes when he hits that fucking rock makes my skin burn; my throat is dry; I'm afraid he's dead. You're already over him, calling out, crying. I push you aside with all my strength, you gasp for air and fall back and away. Sebastian is unconscious. He's pale as death, and the new fine jagged front teeth have split open his bottom lip. He's bleeding.

"Seba," I whisper. My voice calls from far away, strangely resonant. "Can you hear me, Sebastian? It's Dad."

You've crawled into a thicket. You watch me with your light green eyes, while holding the dog by the leash. For some reason, it's showing its teeth and snarling and barking violently. "He's not fucking dead! Anne!" And it's as if by saying your name I prod you into action. You tie the dog to a tree. You lift Sebastian up and begin to stagger down the path with the large limp child over your shoulder. I don't know why, but I don't take him from you, even though you're sinking under his weight. I simply follow you, keeping about five yards between us, while the dog's bark turns into a pitiful whimper as it realizes that it's being left behind.

I clearly remember the first time I heard Anne say her own name. Almost a whisper, while she looked down. She blushed shyly and smiled a little. And then she did something completely unexpected: suddenly, and with great confidence, she leaned over and kissed me deep and long. She really impressed me. I was so touched. I thought she was so cool. I let my hand run through her hair and pulled gently so her head was forced back a little. She closed her eyes and grinned, almost vulgarly. "Anne?" I whispered. The scent from her skin was unbelievably sharp, almost sour.

Five years later we were called to our first adoption interview.

"My name is Anne," she said loud and clear, placing both hands on the back of the chair before finally taking a seat in the small stuffy office. No one had asked for her name. It seemed strange and formal. As if her name was the deciding factor in whether or not she was fit to be a mother. "There's no guarantee that you will get a sweet little baby. You have to imagine that you'll be getting a three-year-old with a harelip and severe mental problems. If you're ready for that then you're ready to adopt," the caseworker said. Anne replied immediately that she was prepared for that.

Much later, when we picked up Sebastian and were sitting on our separate sides of the large king-sized bed in a hotel in

Hanoi and with him between us throwing up, she said suddenly, "His name is Sebastian, and I'm not going to discuss it."

Their names sit like two awls in my main artery: If someone pulled them out, I'd bleed to death in a flash.

You trudge along with Sebastian at least five hundred yards, and I can hear how out of breath you are. You don't say anything. The foliage over us is dense, it's cloudy now, dark and damp where we're walking; I can smell resin and mold and wet grass. Then suddenly you turn off the path and go into the forest. You stagger a few yards and almost trip over a thick gnarled branch, you squat and gently lay the boy down under a tree. Sebastian is chalk white against the dark green moss. You shoo a fly away from his face. I bend down to the child and notice his faint breathing like a fine dust of warm air on my face. I stand up and put my hands on your shoulders. "Look at him," I say, "he's coming back to his old self again. We're going now. We're going, Anne, and before you know it, we'll be near Bulbjerg, and then there's got to be someone there with a fucking car so we can get him to the emergency room."

I lift up Sebastian and place him on my back like a bundle. "Come on," I say. You follow obediently and walk next to me hunched over, exhausted, I imagine, but you don't cry. I tell you that we're almost out of the forest, that I'm certain of it, that we just have to pass through a rosehip hedge and over a rise and then we'll be able to see Bulbjerg and the entire fascinating landscape that surrounds the cliff. Kittiwakes breed out here. Northern fulmars, too, I think. *Fulmar*, what a strange name for a seabird.

"I'm having an affair," I say. You turn your head and look at me, astonished.

"I have a mistress," I say. You knit your brows together, uncomprehending.

"I'm fucking your sister. You understand?" You speed up. "I'm screwing Tine, I can't get enough of her, she gives me head like she's been paid to do it, I can't get enough, I fuck her on the rug at home, I fuck her on the kitchen table, in the bathroom. I take her from behind, up her ass, in our bed…" Suddenly I notice how I'm breathing hard and wheezing. She stops.

"In our bed?" she says. "Up her ass?" she says.

I turn around and look at her. She's clutching at her throat, and swaying back and forth a little. She stares at me a long time, and I can see her nostrils flaring. She shakes her head. Fear and an almost divine purity radiate from her wide-open eyes.

"You're sick," she then whispers.

But quickly her voice becomes loud and shrill, "You're crazy," she cries, pointing at me, she runs backward in front of me, pointing with a straight finger, "YOU SICK BASTARD!" she yells with more rage than I'd imagined; she's ugly and distorted, her movements are mechanical, clumsy, "You disgusting, sick BASTARD!" she shouts, and this is the only thing that comes out of her mouth: sick bastard, disgusting, sick, filthy bastard. And she turns and just runs, she sprints as if the devil were on her heels, and I finally make it to the top and see Bulbjerg towering in the distance. My eyes follow first the soft stretch of coastline, then I look out over the sea, far out, the great wild North Sea, which is grayish-green today and almost completely still. I close my eyes and open them again. There's more wind out here. I want to lie down and surrender to the white light, close my eyes and feel only the wind in the grass, that distinctive whistling sound that the summer wind releases in the grass, and the bumblebees, the grasshoppers, so, so near.

But at that moment Sebastian begins to make small moaning sounds. I take him into my arms and hug him tightly. The bump on his forehead is huge and bluish-red, and a deep gash cuts right across the middle. Blood flows from the light red, exposed flesh. He reaches his hand up and cautiously touches some dried blood on his lip. His tongue glides over the wound, he knits his brows, winces, and calls for his mother.

"Mom ran ahead of us. We have to flag down a car so we can take you to the hospital. You've fallen, Sebastian. The doctor just needs to look at your head. Are you sick to your stomach?" He meekly shakes his head no. I carry him like a baby. His eyes slide shut as I walk. I try to keep him awake. I remember that you're not supposed to sleep when you've hit your head. I retell little stories from his life and ask if he remembers the time we played soccer with the big boys on the field over in the park, and one of them gave him a baseball cap. "And when we were in Tivoli with Mom and Grandma and Aunt Tine, and you ate three cotton candies, and we could see the tower of the town hall when we rode on the roller coaster, and you peed in your pants?" I speak loudly and make sure that I laugh once in a while to startle him; I want to keep him awake at all costs. I jog a bit. Now I see Anne a long way off in the distance on her way down the big hill. She's hunched over walking and reeling in the middle of the road. The many different grasses wave in the wind on all sides, it's incredibly beautiful here. The ocean sparkles far down below, the sky is vast and open. It feels good to be out of the forest, I feel light and comfortable here where one can breathe. I begin to sing to Sebastian. I sing as I begin heading down the hill, down the steep paved road, which is still sticky and soft from the sun. I have a violent urge to race down it; it's not only tempting, but perfectly reasonable to run down a hill like this, yelling, ecstatic, but I don't. I walk and walk toward land again, toward the main road, with both Bulbjerg and the ocean at my back.

Little by little Sebastian becomes livelier and more lucid. I put him on my shoulders so he can see the landscape, and when I look around for Anne again, she's gone. A little while later I make out the sign. Imagine finding a hotdog stand in such a desolate place. I wonder how it stays in business.

Sebastian catches sight of a butterfly and flaps his arms. He asks how long a butterfly lives. The sun comes out for a moment through the clouds and sends a burst of warmth through me. My son is healthy and happy. I have the feeling that things will soon become simple and clear. But when we turn into the parking lot near the stand, the first thing I see is Anne. She's sitting on a bench with a man. The man has his arm around her, and she's got her face buried in his chest, it looks like she's crying. I stop. "Mom," Sebastian says. She lifts her head, trembling, and looks at us for a moment. Then she breaks down again in the man's arms. He has dark curly hair and is very tan. "Anne isn't doing so well," he says. He speaks the local dialect, heavy and droning, the dialect that Anne and Tine dropped long ago.

"Listen, my son hit his head and I need an ambulance right away." The man shakes his head despondently. "A phone," I say. He gets up slowly from the bench. "What kind of a man are you?" he asks. Slowly, slowly he moves toward me. "I'll tell you what kind of a man I am, I'm Anne's husband, and I need to use your phone." I go over to the counter. A strong smell of burnt oil hits me in the face.

"Hell of a husband," he mutters. I lean over the counter and grab the cell phone. But he must have snuck up behind me because when I go to press the numbers, he tears the phone out my hand. He's right up close, his eyes narrow with his upper lip pulling back a little.

"I should beat the shit out of you," he hisses. Sebastian pulls my hair. "Just call," I say, exhausted. Out of nowhere, Anne lets out a yell. I reach for the phone again and try to pry it out of his hand. He lets go and it drops down to the ground and he lays his big hand on my shoulder. "Give me the boy and piss off." I lose my balance and nearly drop Sebastian. He must have pushed me hard. "Dad?" says Sebastian. His voice is weak and well-behaved, he's scared. I turn around and look at Anne.

"Who is this person?" I ask. She gives me a grim look.

"It's Sebastian," she says, and I can tell that this startles the boy, who's still on my shoulders. "Do as he says. Get the fuck out of here."

Sebastian takes hold of my head with both hands, I feel his warm breath all the way down my ear canal. "I want to go home," he whispers.

"Come here, Seba," says Anne getting up. "Come here." She moves closer with outstretched arms. "Come and get an ice cream from Sebastian, he's the one you're named after." Her face is twisted into a crazed grimace.

He looked a lot like an ape, standing there with his broad chest and hairy arms. He stepped forward and pointed suddenly, threatening me with his short fat finger. I walked backward, then started to run. He didn't follow us. When I looked back a little later, I thought I saw him standing in the middle of the road kissing Anne deeply, pulling on her ponytail. I also thought that I could hear her mooing like a cow, maybe it was him, I'm not sure. We reached the main road. Sebastian was silent and stiff. I didn't say anything either. Tine's white breasts and the small dark nipples. The fat finger pointing right at the soft spot between my eyes. I was sweating heavily and was startled when I heard myself gasp.

It was nearly dark before a car finally picked us up. Sebastian was for the most part fine. The doctor examined him, the nurse tried to make him to laugh. He didn't say a word. They glued his wound together, and sent us home. You were sitting in the dark by the window when we got back to the summerhouse late that evening. You hadn't even fetched the dog.

It was completely still on the terrace in front of the house where Iben was sitting on a bench with her back against the wall enjoying watching the children bounce on the trampoline. She could hear Peter shouting something, making the children squeal with delight. It was such a beautiful day. The September sun crashed down from a cloudless sky. The cat snuck under the bench. They had all sat there eating breakfast a little while ago, and now Kamilla was inside doing the dishes with the girls. Iben closed her eyes and leaned her head back. She remembered a sad and pretty song that always made her cry with joy when she was young. She whistled the opening lines to herself. Then someone was pulling on her sleeves. It was her son wanting to go down and throw stones into the pond at the far end of the yard. She got up and took him by the hand.

Mosquitoes swarmed over the water. She threw a stick in and told the boy that it was now sailing out into the wide world. But the boy replied that it would never come up from that mudhole again. The girl bounced light as a feather up and down on the trampoline. Peter stood near them smoking. Then Kamilla came out on the balcony with a camera. "Smile!" she shouted. Iben and the boy went over to the others, and then all four of them looked up at her. Peter made the children say *cheese*. Kamilla suggested that they go to the bakery to get some pastries.

They put both children in the carriage. The neighborhood was abuzz with Sunday and late summer; people were busy with garden work and afternoon coffee, a group of teenagers played ball, and some younger boys sat in an apple tree and threw rocks at a small group of girls playing hopscotch. The strong orange afternoon light made everything look clear and almost surreal. Peter's brown eyes shone like illuminated stained glass, and she began to wonder about the yellow spot she thought he had in his left eye, which he definitely once had, but that she hadn't noticed in a long time.

"What a day!" he said, pushing her to the side so he could take over the carriage. "And here we are taking a stroll," she said. "Yeah," he said, "here we are taking a stroll."

The bakery was closed so they had to go to the gas station at the other end of town. They walked in step side by side. They talked a little about the older girls. Iben said they should probably start thinking about birth control for the oldest one. "For Christ's sake, she's only fourteen!" Peter said, raising his voice. Iben told him that the youngest one was still lagging behind in school and was getting terrible grades. "You have to go over her homework with her more," she said. Peter snorted, "Birth control!" She looked up at a poplar tree and caught sight of a squirrel. She counted to ten slowly to herself. A large BMW was parking in front of them. "They've got too much fucking money around here," said Peter, stepping testily to the side as the car backed over a large puddle. "We'll never have that problem," she said. Then he stopped at the hotdog stand and got the children hotdogs with ketchup and relish. He bought a hamburger for himself. She had a bite, and he wiped ketchup from her cheek. They shared a pint of chocolate milk. "Like the old days," he said, with his mouth full of relish, "before we learned how to cook." "When we lived on fried cod roe," she said. "With mushy potatoes," he said. "Yeah, and that was because you insisted on cooking them in the down comforter, like your mother taught you, but you can only make rice pudding that way." Then the girl began to cry and he pulled her out of the carriage and swung her around. That scared her and she gulped down most of her hotdog. Iben hurried to walk ahead. It was such a beautiful day.

They stood in the convenience store at the gas station, each with a child in their arms—he wanted a lemon pound cake and she, a marzipan cake. They ended up buying both. On the way back, he wanted to have a cigarette. "Why didn't you buy some yourself?" she asked. "I didn't think of it," he answered, as she rooted around in her pocket for a match. She sighed. He began to hum an old pop song, and soon he was screaming it at the top of his lungs. People in their gardens turned to look at them. The girl fell asleep. The light grew deeper in color, redder, and she said she heard that at some point people who are dying blaze up, become their old selves again, full of energy, so that their loved ones almost think that they're about to come around, and then suddenly they die; this feels unexpected and so it comes as a big shock. Peter threw his cigarette over the wrought iron gate. "That's what they deserve," he said. "Did you hear anything I said?" she asked. "Rich bastards!" he yelled. The man passing them on the path in a polo shirt and tan trousers stared condescendingly, first at them, then at the worn carriage, which they had bought for the older girls.

When they got back to Kamilla's house, the girls came bounding up the garden path. The eldest smacked the garden gate into Peter's stomach. Kamilla came walking across the lawn with a coffee pot. "They're going down to get the dog at Madsen's," she said. "What the hell is the dog doing at Madsen's?" Peter asked. "They used to have a dog salon, Peter. You know that Mom and Dad always got Bonnie trimmed there." Peter looked at Iben with an expression that made her laugh hysterically. "Peter! It's a terrier," she said, miffed. "It needs to be trimmed once in a while, and Madsen does it on the cheap." Iben took the boy out of the carriage and walked a little ways away. "A terrier!" she heard him say, and she began to titter and pushed herself forward in order not to laugh outright. She could feel that Peter was watching her. She heard him laugh loudly. "You two!" said Kamilla, who was disappointed about the pastries. She had been looking forward to cream puffs. And it was cold now, even though all three of them were wrapped in down blankets. Iben still didn't dare to look at Peter. Laughter stirred in her throat, for a moment she was afraid she'd begin to cry. The boy stuffed a large piece of lemon pound cake in his mouth. The girl sighed in her sleep. Peter said, "Can you take the girls next weekend? Dorte's parents are coming to stay with us." "Poor you," said Iben, wiping the boy's mouth. He was busy pulling apart a dead flower. A cold wind blew the petals onto the grass. She had finally gotten control of herself. "I thought you were coming to Aunt Janne's birthday on Sunday," said Kamilla. "Sorry," said Peter, shooting Iben a look, who suddenly had to put her hand to her mouth to hold back the laughter. Kamilla leaned back in the chair. "How long have you two been divorced?" she asked. "Seven years in November," said Iben, looking at Peter. "Isn't that right?" He nodded. "Seven years in November," he repeated. The sun shone right in his eyes, and she finally caught sight of the yellow spot in the brown. She felt strangely relieved. She knew it was there somewhere.

THE HONEYMOON

It was Tim's eagerness and boundless spontaneity that got them to set out up the mountain in the midday heat. The Greek landscape, which Eva never cared for, appeared more hostile and parched than ever. The stone pines and wild olive trees dangled out over the steep slopes like helpless mourners, and the pervasive smell of thyme made her nauseous. But Tim wanted to see the women's town, Olympus, which lay at the top of the mountain. And so they drove up in the old, beat-up car he had rented from an American woman who reminded him of his mother with her flowing robes and wrinkled, sun-ravaged skin. The muffler rattled over the gravel road. Eva kissed Tim on the neck. He looked at her. Their faces lit up in radiant, knowing smiles. He let his hand glide up under her yellow cotton dress. Her thighs were warm and damp from sweat. But a little while later, when Eva insisted they pull over, Tim took a picture of her bare bottom as she squatted to pee; she jumped up and ran after him, trying to pull the camera out of his hands, she was furious, but he just laughed and ran up the road, managing to take another picture: She's standing, legs apart, shouting with her mouth wide open as she points menacingly at him. Behind her you can see a silvery-green wild tangle of vegetation and the dusty black car. The left side of her face is lit up by the sun. One of her straps has slid down her shoulder.

She got in the car, slammed the door, and swore that starting now she would not talk to him for at least half an hour. He shook his head and sped up. He laughed and said she was a Fury. He said he loved her. But Eva would not give in. They were both thirsty, but they had finished their water long ago. Small stones from the road kept shooting up and hitting the car as they drove and after a while she began to feel crazy from the racket.

Then suddenly a man stepped out of the bushes and stood in the middle of the road with his arms raised over his head like a priest calling for prayers and devotion. His voice rose and fell, almost as though he were singing. His full beard was impressive. Long matted hair stood out like a lion's mane around his reddish-brown, dirty face. His eyes shone wildly from their deep sockets. He was tall and dressed in rags. He had obviously been living out in the wild for a long time. A savage. Eva had read somewhere that you can find out everything about a person by how he or she reacts in a panic situation. Tim did something strange: he sped up and drove right at the man. The man just stood there. Eva thought she heard herself scream. Then Tim slammed on the brakes and the car swerved to the side. The man was hit, but apparently not seriously; he raised his voice and moved toward the two in the car.

"And they inclos'd my infinite brain into a narrow circle.

And sunk my heart into the Abyss, a red round globe hot burning."

Eva rolled the window up and locked the door. Something fluttered in her field of vision. She thought she heard herself whimper. Tim tore his door open and got out, agitated. He walked toward the man, who continued to stretch his arms toward the sky. Tim screamed in his face. The man then started to move. And now the fluttering was right in front of her, his ragged sleeves, the hands gesticulating madly, and then that terrifying face, the burning insistent eyes that were almost ice blue. He pressed his nose against the windshield. She turned her head away. He scratched on the glass with his long curled nails.

"Stampt with my signet are the swarthy children of the sun;
They are obedient, they resist not, they obey the scourge:
Their daughters worship terrors and obey the violent."

Eva could see that Tim had gotten ahold of him and was trying to pull him back. The man shook him off with the same ease a cow swishes a fly away from its anus, and she freed herself from the seat belt and crawled over to Tim's seat, but in the next moment, the door opened from the outside, and she saw that the man was now shoving himself, torso first, into the car, shoving her in front of him, squeezing and pushing. An acrid, disgusting smell of unclean human being, of excrement and urine, filled her nose. She fumbled desperately with the lock, but he got ahold of her cheeks, forcing her head right up against his. He rested his forehead against hers. She shook her head hysterically, and now she was completely certain that she heard herself howling.

"By gratified desire by strong devouring appetite she fills
Los with ambitious fury that his race shall all devour."

He pumped and hissed the words out of his stinking mouth. She could hear Tim yelling something incomprehensible in the background, and she caught a glimpse of his eyes; now the rage was replaced by an empty anxiety. The man groped her all over her body.

He felt her with his hands, grabbed her thighs and squeezed them, shook her shoulders, pulled on her earlobes, scratched her scalp, stuck his thumbs up her nostrils, his stiff dry hands went all over while she howled and lashed out and tried to break free of the colossally large person. And then suddenly he let go of her. He let her go and looked at her almost tenderly. "Follow me O my flocks we will now descend into the valley," he whispered. He lifted his index finger up in front of her, in warning, or simply to mark the stillness. Then he gave a slight arrogant nod and pushed himself snorting out of the car. His gaze burned in her eyes. Tim stood glaring with a stick in his hand. The man straightened himself up, breathed in deeply and noisily, then exhaled lightly into a slouch. He walked away from the road and up the mountain until he vanished behind a yellowish-gray, jutting cliff. They both noticed that he limped. Eva could not move. One thought stood still in her head: She was certain that the man recited William Blake, the English poet. As a teenager, she had learned some of his poems by heart. She recognized a couple of stanzas from "Visions of the Daughters of Albion." But, she thought, and her thoughts were clear and cool, he had quoted randomly and out of sequence. When she lifted her head and looked, Tim had thrown the stick away and was rushing over to pull her out of the car. When he got hold of her hands and called her name, she forgot about the thought she'd just had; hysteria crashed over her like a tall, dark wave.

She hit him in the face when he tried to hold her. She uttered small sounds of despair that made him think of young birds, chicks, and mice. She headed back to the car, hunched over with her arms dangling from her body. He stood puzzled in the middle of the road, noticing how distorted her face looked.

From where he stood he couldn't tell if it was because she was crying. Her hair was a mess. He gasped. A stab of pain ran up through the back of his head. Then he got in and sat down next to her. He eased the car back onto the road, and drove on in silence. The man's smell still hung in the air. She kept on brushing off her clothes and rubbing her skin. Tim put his hand on her knee. A powerful inner shaking made her start to tremble. Tim quickly figured out that it would be longer to go back to the coast and the hotel than to Olympus, and so he continued on upward. The car rumbled and grumbled, and small rocks hit the car with a noise that to her now sounded like a volley of gunfire. She stuck her fingers in her ears and doubled over. Tim glanced nervously at her. But no matter how hard he tried, he could not think of anything to say that wouldn't sound foolish. He was relieved when at last he caught sight of the town. A large parking lot functioned as a sort of city gate. Relaxed tourists sauntered between the souvenir stands eating ice cream. "We're here," said Tim, gently removing Eva's hands from her ears. He had to lift her out of the car. She didn't resist. He could not help noticing how compliant she was.

The town was smaller than he thought it would be, and it had a strange atmosphere. He felt they were being laughed at from inside the dark restaurants, whispered about and pointed at behind their backs. He asked Eva if she wanted anything to drink. She shook her head. They walked like sleepwalkers through the town, he with his arm around her back, she with a bent head and slack arms. They passed a small, whitewashed church and were suddenly at the town's outskirts. A flat area of sun-dried grass opened out in a half circle toward the bright horizon. And suddenly he could see the sea far below. Primitive houses and huts were scattered further down the mountain, and then it suddenly dropped off. A herd of goats grazed with tinkling bells around their necks. The light was sharp and white. And it was dizzyingly steep. She sat down in the grass. She lay down. She closed her eyes. He shook her lightly. She didn't move. A little while later, she looked like she was sleeping, her mouth was open, she had turned her head to the side, and bent one knee. Small sweat beads broke out on her forehead, she was ash-gray. He shook her. When she didn't respond, he let her rest and decided to go find something to drink. He found his way back to the small gravel road that was the main street of the town. The restaurants and taverns stood side by side. The town was slowly waking up after the siesta. Clearly the women had all the power here. He and Eva had read about it. The whole island functioned as a matriarchy; the order of succession went from mother to daughter. The women owned everything, whatever was worth owning. And here he saw it in practice; in any case, that's what he thought. The women ran the businesses with an iron fist. They gathered outside the shops and bars, standing in small groups with their hands on their hips, and, with agitated hand movements and loud shouts, they bossed around the older boys and men who had snuck in to take a break from working. Old men with little children on their hips, boys in the middle of sweeping or carrying in goods, men dragging heavy bags home from the shops, men sweeping the stone steps, men washing dishes in the kitchens of the restaurants, whose eyes he met through the open windows. The women frightened him. There was a self-confidence in their eyes when they looked at him that he'd never seen in women before. A clear strong energy, a power, and the deep satisfaction that that power gives. Without under-tones of either anger or vindictiveness. No disdain or cloying sweetness. No hint of a wish to be accepted, acknowledged, or liked. Now he was completely sure that they were laughing at him. He was starving and went into a tavern. He ordered wine, bread, and small sour dolmas. A few children played noisily at the back of the bar. The waiter was apparently their father. Five or six elderly women sat on the veranda facing the valley, drinking coffee. They spread themselves over the chairs, one had her legs up, and they chatted away. Tim could not stop himself from scowling at them. They stared back unabashed. He felt strangely exposed. The oldest one yelled to the young waiter. He chased the children out and brought cake and ice water to the women. Tim ate his food quickly and left a good tip. It was a relief to get out in the warm air again. He bought a bottle of water, a postcard of the church, and a package of crackers. Three young women stood in the middle of the road with a screaming baby in a stroller. They looked him up and down shamelessly as he walked by. One of them gave a low whistle, and when he turned, all three smiled lewdly at him, pointing and laughing out loud. He suddenly had the feeling that it was a kind of play the whole town performed in honor of the visitors, putting on this performance about the matriarchy, everyone playing their parts so that the gaping tourists got what they came for. The exotic. Women over men. It was simply a lie. The men thrashed their wives in the evening when the town was quiet and dark, the girls made dinner, cleaned, allowed themselves to be impregnated, allowed themselves to be worn. The men gambled their money away at the card table at night. The thought reassured him. And filled him with shame. He walked back to Eva.

But Eva was gone. There was still a faint outline of her body in the grass. He didn't see her anywhere. He dropped his bag of water and crackers and climbed down to the plateau that stretched out and then down toward the water. He went all the way to the edge and looked down the steep slope of the mountain. It was at least five hundred yards down. Far below, a little strip of sandy beach and large waves hurtling themselves toward the land. The enormous sky. The strong, frightening urge to let oneself fall. Suddenly in his head flashed an image of the tall, stinking man waving his arms and yelling. Tim stepped back with a sinking heart, and when he turned his head to the side, he glimpsed a little yellow spot moving slowly down the bare cliff.

She was awakened by a boy poking her with a stick. She had no idea where she was. The boy ran away giggling. And then she noticed it, the itchiness over her entire body, prickly and stinging, unbearable, as if she were covered in itching powder or attacked by vermin. She scratched herself in a panic, but that didn't help. She pulled her dress up and scratched her thighs and stomach. She began running. She tore through the waving grass, she could smell thyme, she slipped and got up again, she rushed forward. And when she saw the sea, sparkling and wild far below her, she tore off her clothes and began to crawl down the impassable cliff. There was almost nothing to grab onto. Here and there were small tufts of something that looked like heather or crowberry. Small rises on the cliff where she could place her feet. It was windy out there, and the wind slipped over her body, cooling her itchy skin. She had to get into the water. She had to dunk under the blue water, the blue water would wash her clean. She had to drink the salt water and rinse her mouth and throat. She had to disappear in the water, the water would free her. There was a sound like voices being carried away on the wind. Then she slipped and missed the foothold. Stones and dirt went rattling down over the mountain. She caught hold of a gnarled branch and searched desperately with her feet for something to stand on. Her arms shook. Then she swung her body up and placed her feet directly on the wall of the cliff. She tried to put the weight on her thighs. That's how she stood, like a V sticking out from the cliff, clinging to the knotty branch, which, as it was being pulled, was becoming more of a root than a branch, when, from above, Tim reached his arm down and grabbed her wrist. This startled her, her feet slid off the cliff and kicked desperately in the air. A young Greek man grabbed her free hand, and the two men pulled her up with great difficulty onto the narrow ledge they were standing on. The man uncoiled a rope and tied it around her. They carefully lifted her up, tilting sideways. The man walked like a mountain goat on the cliffs. Tim was pale and wet with sweat. He kept his eyes on the passing fleecy clouds that sailed over the mountaintop. The rope bit into Eva's waist and she cried from the pain. With the man's help they were able to get up to something that resembled a path, and for the last part of the way, the man bore her on his back. "She's crazy, she's crazy," he kept saying, shaking his head. Eva laid her head against his hair. It was warm and smelled of salt.

Tim pulled the naked woman behind him through the town to the parking lot. People came out of their houses and lined up to watch them. They whispered and pointed, and a piercing look from an older woman's black eyes made him lower his gaze. "Hurry up for Christ's sake," he hissed. The crowd followed them. They watched how he looked for his car keys, how he shoved Eva into the backseat and slammed the door. They watched how he was unable to get the car started, they heard him swear, and they saw him finally start up the car and back out, raising the dust. They saw him drive away from the town at high speed. And he was about to throw up from exhaustion when he heard Eva humming with an almost childlike, clear voice.

Much later, in the middle of the night, after he'd washed her with cold water from the faucet in the cheap hotel room, after he had gotten her to drink both wine and water, after he had fed her small pieces of goat cheese and bread, after he had wrapped her up in a blanket, a column of irritation and disgust rose up inside him, a disgust directed at her sunburned skin and her almost pleading, simple-minded eyes that kept on searching for his eyes, and the hand she reached out for him that he kept stuffing back under the blanket, until suddenly she got up, letting the blanket slip down onto the floor. Then she did something strange: She shoved him down on the bed and lay over his knees. She begged him to hit her. And he hit her. He hit so that you could hear the slap. She whimpered and groaned. He kept on hitting. And when he got tired, she fetched his belt. She got on all fours, and he let it flick over her back. He cried. He stuck his hand up between her legs to feel how wet she was. Still those pleading eyes. He grabbed her hair. Her back was bloody. A gurgling sound came from somewhere deep inside his throat. And before he could get his pants all the way off, he emptied himself over her feet. She let herself slide down onto her back, and looked up at the ceiling, smiling. A distant, sheepish smile. Outside, it sounded like the cicadas' song was rising. Then he heard her whisper, "We will now descend into the valley."

BLACKCURRANT

As long as there were berries on the bushes, we'd continue to pick them. That's what we agreed on. Helle didn't say a word, and so I was silent too. The sun baked. You could see the cows in the field beyond the garden. We sat on the ground surrounded by shrubs, it was the middle of the day and I was afraid of getting a tick. Our hands were blue and we had already filled an entire pail. There were enough for many jars of jam, and I thought about how wonderful it would be to stand in the kitchen, in the sweet scent from the blackcurrant jam, taking turns skimming it. We'd talk then. There was so much we hadn't had the chance to talk about. I wondered how I should prepare the chicken we bought at the grocery store. I wondered if Helle would soon be tired of picking berries and we could go in and have coffee. But she wasn't getting tired. She dried the sweat off her forehead with the back of her hand, squinted her eyes toward the sun, but then continued. I looked at the tattoo on her upper arm. A faded rose. She got it a long time ago. I was with her that night, we were drunk and she yelled out in pain each time the tattoo artist pricked her skin with the needle. But afterwards we had a beer with him; Helle dried her tears and gave him a kiss right on the mouth.

I remember thinking that it didn't seem like her at all, either to do something as wild as getting a tattoo, or to kiss a man right on the mouth like that. But of course we were drunk. We were often drunk back then. Afterwards, we bought some fresh morning buns, and rode our bikes to the beach and sat there watching the sun rise, and I tore off all my clothes and ran into the water and pretended I was drowning, but Helle was already walking away. I yelled after her, but she didn't stop, and I saw her stagger up over the dunes and disappear. Then I cried. I sat and cried and shivered and got sand in my eyes and under my dress. But of course I was drunk. I don't remember how I got home, and a few days went by before Helle called, but we never spoke about it, why she left without saying good-bye.

Helle pulls the pail toward her and crawls over to the other side of the bush. I attempt to pull a handful of berries off the stem to get around picking them one by one, but they just smear in my hand and I lose most of them. I'm thirsty. I can hear the neighbor driving the tractor back around the barn. He's probably going in for lunch now. There's a sheep that bleats somewhere. I pick at a scab on my knee and look over at Helle's dark head. Her hair is matted. "I'm thirsty," I say. But Helle doesn't answer. A bit later I get up; my legs hurt from having squatted so long, and one of my hands is asleep. It is really boiling hot. Red spots dance in front of my eyes, and for a moment I'm so dizzy that I think I might faint. I turn to look at Helle, but she's still bending over the bush; I can see her hands working fast and steady, the berries nearly flying through the air as she tosses them into the pail.

Once I loved a man passionately. It was a couple of years after Helle got tattooed; he was red-haired and had close-set eyes.

He was so gifted that when he spoke, I thought I was the luckiest person in the world: his words were like colorful pieces of gum wrappers floating inside my head, and my heart lifted up, and I was so light, and I looked at him and I could almost feel my pupils enlarging so I could suck him and his whole brilliantly colored language right in. I begin thinking about this as I walk through the house. And as I drink water from the faucet in the kitchen, I think about him, about his soft fingertips running over my face. Although his fingers never ran over my face—I don't know if he even loved me—anyway we never got that far. I open the refrigerator and look at the chicken. It's big and pale, I have no idea what to do with it. I wonder what became of that man. But we have onions and tomatoes so I can simply throw the whole thing in the oven. I sit down on a stool, and at the same moment I hear Helle come in through the door to the garden. She puts down the pail on the kitchen counter and goes into the bathroom. It sounds like she's splashing water on her face. "Helle?" I shout. She doesn't answer. She turns off the water, it's quiet. I start removing leaves and small twigs from the berries, while listening to figure out what she's doing. But I only hear the neighbor on the road driving by on the tractor, or it could be his son because the neighbor usually rests after lunch. And suddenly I too am overwhelmed by fatigue. On the way into my room I carefully open the door to Helle's room. She's lying on the bed, staring up at the ceiling. I see her chest rising and falling, but otherwise she looks like she's dead.

I slip under my blanket. I think about the man's eyes, the light that shone from them. I see the faded rose on Helle's arm clearly in my mind. And then I must have fallen asleep.

The next thing I remember, Helle is standing in the doorway. She has the chicken in her arms. When I look her in the eye, she turns on her heels and walks away. She looks confused. For a moment, I think it's a dream. But when I stumble into the kitchen, she's standing at the window looking at the neighbor's son. He's walking down the dirt road pulling a black sheep with him.

Then Helle takes some onions out and begins to peel them. "Are you hungry?" I ask. She takes a knife out of the drawer and cuts the onions in quarters. Then I rinse the tomatoes and turn on the radio. Hard rock is playing, but I leave it on. I try to slice the tomatoes so that all the slices are the same size. Helle turns on the oven and places the chicken on the counter in front of me. But I pretend not to get the hint and instead put some water on for coffee. She's sat down on the stool. I turn up the radio and hand her a cup of coffee when it's ready. I look into her blue eyes and keep looking until she looks down. I reach out and carefully touch the rose on her arm. "What's the matter, Helle?" I ask.

We never cooked that chicken. I sauté the tomatoes and onions in a pan, and we eat them with rye bread. Helle has a tremendous appetite. She gets up several times during the meal and opens the refrigerator. She takes out cheese and sausages. She stuffs herself. After this she opens the box of chocolates I got from my grandmother and eats half of it. I just watch her eat. The neighbor drives the tractor out, and now I see clearly that it's him. I get up and go over to the window and he waves to me when he drives by. We've always had good relations, he and his wife are both friendly and helpful. Then Helle washes the dishes and goes back to her room. I start rinsing the blackcurrants. I boil them and measure the sugar. I turn off the radio and enjoy the sounds from the garden flowing in through the open window, the birds chirp and a soft breeze whispers in the large elm. Dusk creeps over the garden and rises like a blue shadow. I scald the glasses then pour in the jam. I lick my sticky fingers. And think about another man I have known. He was dark and short and stocky and had gentle eyes. His skin was so soft that I was surprised each time I touched him. We clung to each other. He made me laugh at things that weren't even funny. I made him long for me wildly, just by walking to the store for cigarettes. I remember every inch of his body. Every little hair growing on his toes. And when I close the door to the garden behind me and gather Helle's green jacket around me, I think about his voice. About what he said to me when he left. We don't have words for everything. It was just that there was someone somewhere else. The gravel crunches under my wooden clogs. I turn left at the road and see that there's a light on in the stable. But the neighbor must have gone to sleep long ago. A sheep bleats loudly. I can't stop myself from opening the door a little and peeking in. The few cows in there look as if they're sick. There's a sharp scent of manure and ammonia. And there, in the narrow path between the stalls, I see the neighbor's son on his knees. He's holding on tightly to the black sheep's wool. And he pushes his groin hard into the animal's backside. The sheep bleats loudly. He lifts his head backward. And as he rattles out a cry like a howl, I see that he has braces on his teeth. Train tracks. I hold onto the doorframe with both hands and shove myself out backward.

At home, Helle has probably already fallen asleep. I sit down in the kitchen and eat jam with a spoon. It's still warm. Helle could've said something before. That she's pregnant and will not have the child. As if I could read her mind. The jam looks almost black now.

The next morning the chicken is still lying on the kitchen counter. It's beginning to smell. I pick it up and carry it all the way across the garden and up to the road. There I let it drop down into the garbage container. Then I wave to the neighbor and his sweet wife, who are now just backing out of their driveway.

They're probably going out shopping.

TORBEN AND MARIA

What can you say about Maria? That her hair is blonde and dark at the roots? That she loves roast pork with cracklings? That as a child she loved to look out at the flat fields at dusk in February? Her eyes rested there, under the low sky, in the gray gray light, until it got so dark that she could see only her face reflected on the window, the green lamp on the table behind her, and all the way back to her mother, leaning against the door smoking.

The window, a black mirror.

Maria.

She hits her small child, until the screaming stops. It's a boy and his name is Torben. Not many people call their sons that any more. Ah, Maria! You can say this about her: "She gave her son the name Torben."

Soon he'll be two. He's a little weakling, and there's nothing special about him.

They're walking down the pedestrian street. Torben and Maria. They're holding hands. They stop at the fountain. Maria sits down on a bench and Torben runs under the chestnut trees. They're in bloom now and very beautiful. He scares up a flock of pigeons, then finds a little black rock. He takes his time with a piece of gum that has been trampled in the grass.

Meanwhile, Maria's phone rings. It's Bjørn.

"We're waiting for you, where the fuck are you, asshole?"

Bjørn is held up. Maria sighs and turns to look for Torben. He's in the middle of a conversation with two young women. They smile and gesticulate. Torben shows them something. They bend down to get a closer look, and both laugh. One pats him on the head. Then they wave good-bye and cut across the lawn. Torben watches them until they disappear. A fly crawls across his forehead.

Maria lights a cigarette and calls him over. He darts back to his mother.

"What a good boy," says an older man who's sitting beside Maria on the bench. "Nowadays kids never do what they're told."

Maria pulls Torben up onto her lap. He shows her the black rock. The man smiles and says, "Hello there little friend." Torben hides his face in Maria's neck.

Then Bjørn arrives out of breath. Maria shakes her head with defeat and starts walking. Bjørn puts Torben on his shoulders.

Bjørn is Maria's brother. They're all going to eat at the restaurant in the train station where you can get roast pork. Bjørn carries Torben the whole way through town.

"Why are you so late, you asshole?"

"Business."

"Business, my ass."

"Really. Cell phones. We made a killing."

"Who's we?"

"Me and Rock."

"You better stay away from Rock."

"Chill the fuck out."

"Stay away from him."

"But he has connections."

"Like hell he does!"

"Chill out. He doesn't give a damn about seeing Torben. You know Rock."

Maria shoots him a furious look. Torben sings, "Bah, bah, black sheep," as well as he can.

"Stop SINGING, Torben!"

"Why can't the kid sing?"

"Because he can't."

Bjørn shrugs.

"You're insane," he says and sings along. He doesn't know the song, and sings both out of tune and way too loud. Torben looks frightened and keeps silent. Meanwhile, Maria crosses to the other sidewalk. Bjørn takes Torben under his arm and cuts to the other side.

"Get your shit together," he yells. "What the hell's wrong with you?"

They eat roast pork and drink Diet Coke. Torben has a hot-dog and french fries. He barely reaches the table. They eat in silence. Then Maria notices the chewing gum stuck to Torben's left palm.

"You pig," she hisses, trying to peel it off.

It won't come off. She turns red and grabs Torben's wrist, squeezing it. Torben stares off into the distance. Maria yanks his arm so hard he bangs his head on the corner of the table.

"Leave the boy alone," Bjørn says with food in his mouth. "Maria!"

She lets him go. Torben continues to stare off into the distance.

"Do you beat him?" Bjørn asks, cleaning the meat and red cabbage off his teeth with his tongue. Maria narrows her eyes and looks at him.

"Stay away from Rock, okay?"

She pushes her plate away. She's eaten everything, even the little sprig of parsley decorating the potatoes. There's almost no trace of sauce left. Torben accidentally knocks over his Coke. Bjørn wipes it up with a napkin.

"Chill the fuck out Maria, he's just a kid."

"He's going to be two in a month."

"That's pretty fucking young."

"Retard."

Then they leave. Delicate pink clouds drift through the sky. Torben and Maria hold hands. They walk up the pedestrian street. Bjørn stops. He needs to go the other way. He's going to meet Rock to buy some weed and talk business.

"Fuck you, Bjørn," Maria says, marching off with Torben.

Bjørn stands there a moment watching them. That stout young woman in black pants and a white top. The blonde hair that's dark at the roots. The boy in the red shorts and T-shirt. He shakes his head and turns around. He sticks his hands in his pockets and walks back around City Hall. He decides to walk all the way to the north end of the city where Rock lives since it's such a fine spring evening. The light is amazing, almost blue and milky now; a black bird sings nearby.

Maria hits her little child. Her son, Torben. She beats him. She hurls him into the wall. She kicks him when he crawls under the dining table. She slaps his face if he picks his nose. She shakes him when he falls asleep on the couch. She ties him to the bars of the crib. Though there's no need to. He always lies there without moving.

"You should hit him on the butt so he doesn't get any marks," her mother says. "Otherwise you'll have the daycare people coming after you."

And she's probably right. They're beginning to wonder. Torben is so shy. But he's also violent. He hits the other children when they come near him. He bites. And he often has bumps and bruises on his body and head. They've talked it over with each other. But on the other hand, Maria seems okay. You can't be too quick to judge people. Children at that age are accident-prone, they're always stumbling and falling and hurting themselves.

But actually, Torben isn't a likeable child. He's not cute. He doesn't shine. In fact, he's completely graceless, ugly, and snot-nosed. He's the kind of child you simply want to be rid of, if you're being honest. There's a difference between children, it's just that way. And maybe that's why no one in daycare really notices Torben's bruises. No one really likes him. Maybe that's why.

Maria locks the door and turns on the light in the hallway. She rummages around for the remote and turns on the TV. The living room is dark. With a sigh, she sinks into the couch. Torben crawls up to her. She strokes his head absentmindedly, he snuggles up to her breast. They watch a program about Africa's coastlines. Torben quickly falls asleep, and Maria carries him into the bedroom. Then she huddles on one end of the large caramel-colored couch with a soda and cigarettes and sits there until long after midnight.

Ah, Maria.

Bjørn is your brother, Torben, your son.

I'm Rock.

Do you remember when we first met? You told me about the flat fields at dusk, and you let me fondle your breasts. We walked up and down the pedestrian street for hours. And you let me touch your hair, while you sat with your back against my stomach on a bench by the fountain. We ate roast pork at the train station restaurant. That was a long time ago. You were so…fresh! It was the summer you turned 17. And I, well, I'm an older guy now. You were so restless, didn't want to be tied down. Now you've gotten heavy. I know so much about you. And you shouldn't worry about Torben. I don't care. He's nothing special. I never for a moment think he's mine. Because he is yours, Maria. Do with him what you want. Little kids don't really do anything for me. Bjørn says you're mad at me. That's fine. We've had our time together, and now I'm content just to follow along from a distance. Not an obsession, more for amusement. You're going in circles, Maria, and it amuses me to follow you: the pedestrian street, the anger, the beatings you heap on the boy, all the cheap clothes, the drinking sprees at bars, and the one-night stands.

The pedestrian street, the anger, the beatings.

I know where I've got you now. It suits me fine.

Torben is turning two years old. Maria's mother is there, and Bjørn. They've bought candy and chips and straws for Torben's soda. All four of them are sitting on the couch. The TV is on and Bjørn is helping Torben unwrap the gifts. Then he takes Torben into the bedroom to play with the new car. The women light cigarettes. They hear Bjørn making the sound of an ambulance.

Torben lies on his stomach on the floor and drives the yellow tractor back and forth.

"Torben. Look. I have something else for you."

Bjørn takes a small package from his pocket. It's a snow globe that usually has a Santa inside it. But there's no Santa in this one. There's a little green fir tree. The background is dark blue with stars. Bjørn shows the boy how to make it snow. Torben stares with an open mouth at the fat falling flakes and takes it and tries it himself.

"It's from your father, Torben. Your father."

But Torben isn't listening. He can't get enough of it. He shakes the globe again and again, gaping with wonder at the miracle. Bjørn gets up from the floor and goes into the living room. The mother has made popcorn in the microwave. Bjørn stuffs a handful in his mouth while lighting a cigarette.

"Rock fucking remembered it. I can't believe it."

"What are you talking about?"

"The boy's birthday."

"Oh, piss off."

"He likes the gift."

Maria stops chewing.

"What?"

"The gift from Rock. The kid's crazy about it."

Maria gets up and storms toward Bjørn.

"Stop, Maria," the mother says.

Maria gives Bjørn a hard push when she passes him on her way out of the living room. She yanks the snow globe out of Torben's hand, walks over to the window and opens it. The boy begins bawling. She throws it as hard as she can and watches the little globe smash to pieces when it hits the sidewalk. Torben clings to her pants. She tears herself from him and slams the door to the bedroom on her way back to the living room. She sinks down into the couch next to her mother.

Bjørn gets his jacket and leaves.

The next time Maria and Torben go out to the street, Torben sees the broken snow globe. He wants to pick up the fir tree, but Maria kicks it under a car. Take it easy, Maria, I won't be sending any more gifts to your snot-nosed kid. It was just a little experiment. I wanted to see if I could make you break out of your circle. But that seems impossible. And you walk up and down the pedestrian street, you and Torben, up and down. You sit on the bench by the fountain. Torben runs under the chestnut trees. You talk to Bjørn on the phone. You eat roast pork and fight. At home, you lift up Torben and smash him into the sharp corner of the kitchen counter. The only thing I'm not able to say about you is what you're thinking when you sit on the couch at night.

Maybe you don't even know yourself.

She bought oysters and fresh tuna and smoked salmon. She thought she might also like lobster, but changed her mind—she was so perky and rosy-cheeked and the fishmonger was flirting with her—and finally she settled on crab. It was windy and cold, her bicycle accidentally fell over and the fishmonger came running out to pick it up, and on top of this, he loaded all her bags into the bicycle basket; there seemed to be no end to his helpfulness. He smiled and she laughed, he waved enthusiastically when at last she walked off, reeling under the heavy load. She hurried. She dropped her keys. She saw beauty in the most ugly and dejected face. She threw money around: a huge bouquet of lilies, white wine, red wine, liquor, champagne, mangoes, beef, bread and cake from the city's most expensive bakery. She hauled it all home and took a bath. But she didn't stay in long. She was nearly out of her mind in love. She rubbed moisturizer all over herself, did her hair, and made up her face. She put on her new lingerie, ah, lacy and silky, then the dress and the midnight blue high heels, which she could hardly walk in, but she *did*, she could do anything, and all these objects were so beautifying, precious, *cheering*, and largely the reason for over-drafting her account.

But there was also the visit to the hair salon, the dance lessons, the copper pot, and the organic duvet. Not to mention the couch and the whole collection of music, purchased to make an impression on him. *Him.* He came in the late afternoon, and they stood in the entryway for more than half an hour kissing. At last he was sweating so much it was dripping from his hair, he still had his coat and hat on. Finally she unzipped his pants. They rolled around on the floor in the narrow hallway, and he accidentally ripped her dress to shreds pulling it down over her hips. They were about to faint from excitement. But then it was over so quickly, they couldn't control themselves. She moaned with pleasure, the tears streaming down her cheeks. He couldn't stop kissing her face, her shoulders, her small soft fingers.

Then they were hungry. He turned on the light. She was beaming. They drank heavily as they ate one delicious course after another, but it wasn't *enough*, they were insatiable, it was nearly impossible to wait for *the next time*—as soon as they got up from the floor or couch or bed they wanted to do it *again*, and when they couldn't drink any more coffee or wine, or eat another bite—they were almost unhappy that they had to wait until when they could again...

But what happiness! They couldn't sleep, work, think (except about each other), couldn't eat (except with each other); they had cold sweats and shivered and called each other a minimum of ten times a day. He lost weight. She gained ten pounds. For no apparent reason he came down with three ear infections, she suffered with an itchy rash, then he broke out all over his face, she lost a lot of hair—but none of this worried them, as long as they could rub against each other like a dog humping its owner's leg. They *rubbed*, they pushed and picked and caressed, they tore and scratched and squeezed, they opened like floodgates and unbelievable, enormous waves poured out of them, an old sorrow, a joy, the actual *past* surged out, while they lapped up the other's water, letting themselves be flooded, filling themselves with caresses, kisses, and sweet words.

Now they were really drunk. He fed her whipped cream from the cake. She got a sudden surge of energy, and jumped up to put some music on, shouting, "Now we're going to have gin and tonic!" and they did, she crawled onto his lap, then suddenly he wanted to dance, and this was exciting, they hadn't *danced* together yet, it was thrilling, a *turning point*, hot. In the middle of it they had sex again, this time she was bent over the kitchen counter, a large knife fell and pierced the floor an inch from his foot, the back of her head was resting in a little mound of parmesan cheese, his sleeves soaked up tomato sauce from the cutting board. The music blasted from the loudspeakers. She howled, he hummed. The semen ran thick and white down her inner thighs. She wiped some up with her finger and licked it clean. He was overwhelmed by joy and gratitude. Now it was his turn to nearly whimper. He lifted her up and carried her to the bed. They were drunk, she felt like throwing up, he had to pee, but neither of them wanted to spoil such an unforgettable moment, neither wanted to get up and *abandon* the other. They fell asleep with their shoes on. The next morning they had nasty hangovers. But then it was time for coffee. And that's how it went. Lunch at one of the most exclusive restaurants in the city. More coffee. Then to the movies, holding hands and getting turned on in the dark. Sex in the bathroom of a bar. More coffee. Sleep a little (they didn't *sleep*). Everything all over again, nonstop, for almost five months.

At work, he sat at his desk staring at the phone. He couldn't concentrate, his colleagues smiled at him, he saw her in every face, heard her in all the pop songs, and whenever he closed his eyes, he saw an image of her head thrown back, her face's violent beauty, her mouth open when the orgasm rolled through her body.

It ruined them. They didn't care. They bought a house. Then they wanted to go to Spain. Then New York. They drove through Poland on a motorcycle. They got married in Las Vegas. Then they had a child. And just two weeks after the birth, they were at it again, they simply fucked between the baby's feedings, there were no problems with fatigue or sour breast milk, there was only *them*, wild and giddy, and now, as well, a deep, rapturous *love*, there was nothing they couldn't do together, the world became a place they could easily conquer, lock, stock, and barrel, no expenses spared, or fear that it would all come apart. They felt transformed and continually reassured each other of it: *We have transformed each other*, miraculously, and there was no end to the blessings.

But then, anyway, something happened. He met a man. And that man came closer and closer. Work took them around the country, they were employees in the same firm. It was late summer. They sat in the car listening to music. Closer and closer. All of a sudden his floodgates were opened. It poured. It unfurled. Vague fantasies were thrown into relief. The desire was inevitable. He had never thought that he actually *would*. But this man would. Then he was suddenly on his knees and *took it in*, there at the hotel. A starry sky, everything blinking. To be soft like that, almost round, giving, receiving, like a whore, a child, it nearly tore his mind in pieces, and that was exactly what was so good, so deeply, liberatingly good. He was astonished. He felt fulfilled, when he went from him to her, completely liberated, and the opposite direction, completely vital—he could freely shift between being her man (responsible, loving), the child's father (tender, attentive), and then take his lover's cock in his mouth and do *everything he's told*.

Pure happiness.

And her. She feels it's just getting better and better between them, and she didn't really understand how it *could* get any better. She watched with admiration as he dried himself after showering. She threw her arms around his neck and hugged him. He grabbed her buttocks and sniffed deeply into her hair. They laughed and opened the window so the steam could get out. They went for a walk in the forest. Their child tried to balance on a huge stack of stripped tree trunks. A pheasant ran across the path. It rustled and pulsed on the forest floor; a mild and gray February day. He swung her around, she laughed again. Her hands found their way to his bare back. He kissed her eyes. They were *so happy*. And for a long time, nearly three years, only better and better; the lover brought a friend, and now there were two men to serve; he was busy, but it was completely worth it. He didn't feel in the least bit guilty. Because she inspired strength in him. They loved each other with such intensity that they could only grow together.

But then the child saw her father kissing a man in a passageway. She was coming home from preschool with her grandmother. And the child saw that it wasn't a completely ordinary kiss, because her father and the man went on kissing, but the most disturbing part was that the man was holding the nape of her father's neck as if he were pushing him *down*. The child stood completely still.

In the evening she told her mother, "I saw Daddy kissing a fat man." Her mother laughed. "What kind of nonsense is that?" He was in the kitchen drying the dishes. He froze. "That was probably one of Daddy's friends." Then she tucked the child into bed. He was changing the bulb in the range hood. "Did you hear what she said?" "No, what?" "That she saw you kissing a fat man!" He smiled. "Were you kissing a fat man, honey?" She couldn't stop herself from giggling. He shook his head laughing and began screwing in the bulb. "Kids! It must be some damn Oedipal complex!" They laughed. The bulb lit up white in the range hood. But she became quiet for a moment scraping her nail on the varnish of the counter. She looked at him with tear-filled eyes. "Honey, why are you crying?" He put his arms around her. "Honey, you're crying over nothing?" He stroked her hair. She calmed down, and smelled the pit of his arm: pine forest, earth, warm rain.

He was more careful. No more kissing in the passageway. New meeting places. But still sex. At least once a week. He was dependent on it, he *needed* it. But then his lover called it off. He had found someone else and thought that their relationship had *dried up*. It was hard to hide his disappointment. He laid new flooring in the dining room. That helped. He made love with her frequently. That also helped. Time passed. After awhile their finances were secure. Another baby was born. They helped each other with chores at home, they enjoyed their children, they really made it *work*. Suddenly, one winter evening, when he was still awake working, it came over him. Strong and burning. He drove downtown and parked outside a bar that he knew from his teenage years. He and his friends would amuse themselves laughing excitedly and with condescension at the leather-clad men coming out of there—now he came out of the dark with a tall, middle-aged man, and went to a nearby club that the man was a member of, they undressed, they washed, they found a place to do it, around them were others doing it, there was panting and a smell of sweat, which made him completely delirious.

By chance a few years later she finds the midnight blue shoes at the bottom of the closet while looking for something else. There are coffee stains on them. She caresses them smiling. *That was the day I bought oysters, and he ripped my fancy dress to shreds.* She's naked, rummaging around on a shelf with underwear. It's a big one, and she's happy she has it. He bought it for her, but then realized he also liked having her put it in him. It surprised her, to be doing something like that. That she even enjoyed it. And it had surprised her that he let her do it. But, she thinks shutting the closet door, there is such a *connection* between us. We're marked by each other. Then she puts the shoes on and looks in the mirror. Still beautiful. Her skin is dull and white in the dim light. He's already lying in bed, settled and ready. "You're so wonderful," he whispers pulling her down to him.

That's Anika standing on the dusty platform with her doll in a light blue fabric bassinet lined with a thin blue-dotted plastic. With one hand she holds on tightly to her father's gray flannel pants. With the other, she swings the bassinet back and forth. All the while she stares at a little girl on her mother's hip on the opposite platform. The girl has laid her arms around her mother's neck and is pushing her cheek into her face. Anika and her father have been standing there for a while; the father is reading the newspaper and gives her a distracted answer every time she asks him something. "Is that our train?" He nods. "Is it?" "No…" "Why are you reading the newspaper?" "Hmm…"

They took a taxi to the train station, and Anika sat completely still looking at the back of the driver's fat gray neck. The car smelled bad. Her father spoke in another manner, and laughed strangely when the driver said anything that was apparently funny. She had cried a lot when they were about to leave. The baby spit up down the mother's back. Anika screamed when her father carried her out the door. They are going to see Grandma and Grandpa. Her mother is too tired to come. Anika doesn't think she looks tired. It's her baby sister who sleeps all the time. The father folds up the newspaper and smiles at her. "Do you know what we're going to do when we get to the ferry? We're going to get some ice cream."

A tall, strange man comes smiling toward Anika and her father, and it's obviously someone the father knows, for they greet each other warmly with loud exclamations of surprise, and they both set their suitcases between their legs to shake each other's hand. "This is my daughter," says the father, touching her head, "This is Anika." "Wow," says the man, "the last time I saw her she was in a baby carriage." "Three years old," says the father, "she's three and a half now, and a month ago we had another little girl." The strange man lifts his gaze from Anika, to the father, and then pats him enthusiastically on the shoulder. "Congratulations, old boy, I'm so happy for you! And mother and child are well?" At this point in the conversation, Anika places her bassinet between her legs and puts her hands on her hips. Now she's standing exactly like the two men. She looks up at the strange man's face, and doesn't long any more to return to her mother in the apartment with the yellow curtains and the cat that's almost always lying in the sun on the kitchen floor with half-closed eyes. She has imitated the two men's postures down to the smallest detail, and she looks over at the girl again who is still clinging to her suntanned mother. Stupid little girl. Anika can feel the bassinet against her legs. She makes a large spit bubble that bursts so that her mouth gets wet. She sticks her tongue out at the girl. She feels tall and wide. It feels a little like the time she was at the swimming pool with her mother, the water was cold, she shrieked, but it was nice, and she now shifts to her left foot, exactly as her father has just done, and a wonderful sensation floods through her, something velvety soft and dark, but at the same time, extremely bright. She: a person. She can almost not stand still any more, she wants to hop up and down, she wants to run all the way to the trash can at the other end of the platform, but when she looks at her father and the man, they're saying something with deep murmuring voices, and she notices that they are both standing completely still, as if trapped in their old bearish bodies, so Anika stands like them, rubbing her chin with her thumb and finger, as her father was just doing. That's when the strange man suddenly looks at her. He stops talking mid-sentence, and a smile spreads across his face. He sputters and covers his mouth. Surprised, the father follows his friend's gaze, and then he too burst out in uncontrollable laughter when his eyes scan Anika, stopping first at her legs straddling the bassinet, and then her serious face. Anika hides behind her father. Something burns in her head and stomach. He bends down and picks her up. He tries to get his voice under control. "Don't be sad." He looks at his friend. More laughter. "It's just because it's so funny that you're standing like us, right?" Now his voice begins to shake. "It's funny, don't you think?" The two men let go and laugh loudly. They can't stop. The father with his enormous hand presses her cheek to his face. Anika cries woefully while looking at the girl who at that moment is being lowered down onto the platform by her mother and darts off to climb up onto a bench. Anika cries harder. The laughing ceases. "Sweetie, it's nothing to cry over," says her father. Then the big brown train pulls in between the children, making sizzling, hissing sounds. The father quickly says good-bye to his friend and climbs up into the train, Anika still in his arms. He puts her down on the seat in the compartment. Smiling, he shakes his head. She gets on his lap sniffling, and presses her forehead against the window. She looks at the light blue bassinet left behind on the platform. She doesn't say a word. She can smell her father's pipe tobacco. The window tastes sour. A little black seed that looks like the pupil in her father's eye, the one that squints a bit when he doesn't know what to say, is now planted in her. She feels it rumbling in her stomach, but she doesn't cry. The train pulls out. Fields and woods fly by, far away and green. She doesn't cry.

CANDY

Working our way down the long shopping list, we at last reached the shelves with sweets. We grabbed two bags of mixed candy. You placed them in the large woven market bag, which your mother had bought in Bali. We also grabbed a bar of chocolate, unwrapped it and broke it in half. We devoured the sweet sticky mass. Then we walked up to the checkout and began to unload the groceries onto the conveyor belt. You remembered to put down the chocolate bar wrapper. The young woman at the register threw it in the wastebasket for us. I paid. And then a skinny woman with glasses and gray wispy hair stopped you. "What do you have there?" she asked, pointing at the woven bag. "Oh," you said, "I forgot to put them on the counter." You smiled at the young woman. "I'm sorry." "Sorry isn't good enough," the woman said. "What do you have there?" People watched. "What do you mean? It's candy." "Have you paid for it?" "No, that's what I just said. We forgot to put them on the counter." Red splotches spread across your neck and down your chest. "We'll just pay for them now," I said. "And you're saying that it's candy?" asked the woman. "Yes." Her lips pressed out and down in a nasty smile. "It's stolen goods," she said, "and I couldn't care less about what you've

forgotten or not forgotten. You're coming with me right now."
"What do you mean?" you asked, confused. "Just what I said,"
said the woman, pushing her glasses up. "Excuse me," I said,
"we spend lots of money in this lousy store every day of the
entire summer." I was losing my temper. "And then you scold
my wife like a child for forgetting to pay for two cheap bags
of candy!" I waved one of the packages in her face. "Here!" I
shouted, "Take the money!" and flung a handful of coins on the
counter. The young woman at the register looked miserable.
The money stuck in the conveyer belt where it fed down into
the counter. A German man who was loading his groceries
into a large box tried to wiggle the coins free. It ended with the
young woman stopping the belt. The long line of people with
full shopping carts were asked to check out at another register.
Meanwhile the woman with glasses was saying, "Sir, this is not
about paying now, it's about theft, we have our procedures in
this store, and your wife needs to come with me." She grabbed
your arm. You were on the verge of tears. "Thomas," you whispered. "Don't worry. I'm coming with you," I said, gathering
our things. "Let's get this over with!" I shouted. "Right away!"
"Sir, your wife will be questioned alone. Those are the rules."
"I want to talk to the manager!" I shouted. You looked down
at the floor. She still had your arm, and was now walking off
with you. You didn't resist. I called to the woman at the register. "Get me the manager of this shithole!" I shouted. The
woman looked scared. She rang the bell. I could neither see
you nor the skinny woman. It felt like it took forever before
the manager showed up. Meanwhile I got all worked up over
the fact that the woman had taken great pains to humiliate
you as much as possible by addressing you casually and calling
me sir. The manager appeared to be a good-natured man in his
mid-thirties. In a raised voice, I told him about the situation.

The manager covered himself. "The store detectives are not my responsibility. We use the same procedure for theft in all our stores." "It's not theft," I shouted and almost grabbed the poor man. "Bring me to my wife!" "Unfortunately," the manager said, smiling apologetically, "I'm not allowed to." Then in a rage I threw the bags of candy on the floor and pushed my way through the checkout. I ran down the produce aisle and banged open a metal door behind the meat section. Two men with bloody aprons looked at me surprised. They were putting hamburger meat onto trays. "Where's the OFFICE?" One of the butchers stepped toward me. "It depends on which office you mean." After I explained myself, he shook his head. "Sorry. I can't help you with that." I slammed my hand down on the table and raced for the door farthest back in the building. But that led out to the parking lot. So I ran back into the store. All the way in the back past the shelves of wine I found the door. It was locked. I pounded on it with all my might. I yelled for you. People watched, concerned. Then a security guard with keys jingling on his belt came toward me with quick steps. And when I didn't follow him voluntarily, he grabbed me and pushed me through the store. I yelled. He was strong. He pushed me right out into the street. "Get lost," he said. "You understand?" I kicked a parked car. "You're not going to get away with this," I hissed. "I'm going to report your fucking bullshit." He looked at me arrogantly. "Unfortunately, it's your wife who's going to be reported. Get lost." I stepped toward him and he shoved me and I stumbled over the curb. He hoisted up his pants, making the keys jingle, and went back into the supermarket. I was out of breath. I sweated. A muscular young man poked me on the shoulder. "Hey, did you kick my car? You'd better cut it out." Two others towered behind him. A tall lanky guy and a dark-haired dumpling.

"What do you say guys? Does he have the right to kick my Benz?" "Come on, nothing happened," I said and turned to go. But the dumpling twisted my arm behind my back. "That'll be a hundred bucks." When the others circled me, and asked if they should find the money or kick my ass a little first, I gave in. With my free hand I took some crumpled bills out of my pocket. And the tall lanky one smiled with satisfaction when he took them from me and realized there were one hundred and twenty dollars. "Thank you very much. That'll do." The dumpling shoved me away from him, and that time I fell flat on the ground.

There was a big bloody scrape on my knee. A woman asked if I needed help. The sun blinded me. I noticed a small group of people had gathered around me. I got up and limped away. A young woman muttered, "Look, he's shitfaced," when I passed her. The manager was waiting for me in the store. "Sir, I'll have to ask you to leave at once. The customers are disturbed. We can't take responsibility for that." "Responsibility!" I shook my head and clenched my jaw. I made a show of taking out my phone and calling the police. "Police!" I hissed so that he'd know I wasn't pretending. An impertinent police officer told me that they had already talked to the store detective who reported the theft. My wife would hear from them within the next few days. She might get off with a fine, but there's a chance it'll go on her record, as he said. The manager gently grabbed my arm. "It's all going to work out." I jerked my arm away with a lot of force. It swung backward and knocked over a pyramid-shaped display of cans of clam chowder. There was an enormous crash when the cans knocked each other down. They rolled all over the place. My hand throbbed with pain. A little girl tripped over one of the cans and began screaming. Her father came rushing over. "What the hell are you doing, you idiot?!" Standing a few inches from me, he lifted his fist as if to punch me in the face, but controlled himself when the girl pulled on his leg. "Fucking idiot," he hissed, giving me the evil eye. Then he picked up the child, gave me the finger, and stomped away in his plastic sandals. People glared at me shaking their heads. Some began to restack the cans. The manager grabbed my shoulders. "That's enough," he said with a clenched jaw, "now you've got to go." He gave me a little push. "And don't you dare come back again."

Then you were suddenly standing in front of me, red-eyed and pale. Maybe you had been standing there for a while. In the background I could make out that scrawny woman's strained gloating face. "That's the way out!" The manager raised his voice. Your hand slid in mine. We must have looked defeated. Then we slowly began to walk, and when we got out to the parking lot, you broke down sobbing. I put my arms around you. The air shimmered with heat. We had forgotten to take our groceries and didn't go back for them. A blue Mercedes roared by us, and with the horn going off they shouted and laughed at me through the open windows. I looked at you, and for a moment it was as though I didn't recognize you. Your face reminded me of an old ball that's been kicked to death and left at the edge of a large green field. Misshaped, gray, and flat. I left you standing there and got in the car. I suddenly had no desire to touch you. A little while later you crawled sniffling into the passenger seat. I accelerated and heard you gasp several times because of how fast I was driving as we headed out of town.

THE GREEN DARKNESS
OF THE BIG TREES

Tuesday morning it became clear that autumn was now on its way. There was a new coolness in the air. Drizzles later turned into hail. But between showers there was also intermittent golden sunshine that made the withering leaves light up like copper. A strong scent of damp earth and rot pervaded my morning walk down the familiar walkways and paths. I was melancholic. I thought intensely about death. Summer passes so quickly and who knows if it'll be the last. Because death is tugging at me. And I have to hold on tight with my arms and legs to not give in. It's strange, incomprehensible, that I, who desire life with such strong intensity, have this fierce drive in me. I found myself in the green darkness of the big trees. In this instance, linden trees. They always make me sigh. I put a heart-shaped leaf in my pocket. I sat on the ground, dug my hands down into the loam and closed my eyes. What makes me drift around so restlessly in a world that I'm unable to enter even though it gives me the greatest pleasure when it pierces me? I sat this way for a long time as it poured and the rain ran down my face and I tasted it; I sucked on my dirty fingers. Then, quickly, I made my way over to the old silver maple. My solace, my anchor. Crying, relieved, banging my tired head against the trunk. Leaves fall gently. The sun breaking through. In a flash, everything seemed interconnected as it's meant to be; I watched the shadows of the trees' canopies on the path, and noticed how the wind moved the leaves in the treetops, light falling, shifting quickly between shimmering sunlight and dense darkness, and the sounds of gentle rustling, whispering, and mumbling, all so soothing; my heart about to burst. I am warm and cold, and I was also warm and cold too when the church bells struck ten, and I pressed my mouth against a stray branch, and prayed for my life, and began to walk that Tuesday past the rose beds and the little pond with ducklings. A child lay on her stomach gathering twigs from the water. A young man was absorbed in photographing the greenhouse. The gardener carted manure in a small wheelbarrow. I squatted and stuck my greedy nose into a rose. When I stood up I saw you for the first time. You were leaning against the tool shed with closed eyes. Your skin was very white. You looked happy. Then you opened your eyes, squinting at me. I must have given you a thunderstruck look, because you smiled shyly and made this little movement with your hand, which later I would dream about with such longing, almost a wave but not really, a commanding movement, gracious, apologetic, awkward as a blush. I stood there boring my eyes into your back as you walked away. Your steps were light and springy. I sat down on a bench. And heard the clear incessant sound behind me of the oak tree's acorns hitting the ground with small cracks.

Walking under the big trees brings up an immediate and direct feeling of happiness in me, which I desperately need. Wednesday came, the earth was still damp after the night's rain, a gray haze lay over the garden, and I embraced the gnarled maple, pressed my chest against the trunk, tried to control my breathing. It's always especially bad in the morning. Then out of the corner of my eye I saw something dark and fidgeting stop. Your coat. There you were looking at me. A blue wool hat was pulled down over your ears. You were studying me with your head at an angle. I nodded. Again that wave of your hand, and then you were gone. I didn't continue my stroll through the garden. I didn't lie among the ferns down by the pond. I didn't visit the roses, the wisteria, I didn't gather snowberries from the ground, I didn't kiss the first chestnuts. Instead, I sweated like a horse and went home. Strangely broken-hearted, confused, embarrassed. But with new signs in my body as well, ones that nearly drowned out the coursing blood, the pain around the heart, the sensation of falling, and the usual frightening thoughts that follow. I went home and took my member in my hand. I was warm and cold. I never got tired of rolling the foreskin back and squeezing it forward, my hand racing back and forth. I collapsed into the sticky puddle on the floor. Awhile later it was evening, early and blue. And it turned out that I was already having vivid dreams about you, as if I were hearing your footsteps on the gravel, as if I were touching the swinging ball of your blue hat. I woke up in the middle of the night because I was freezing, and it hit me for the first time that you must've thought I was mentally ill. Who would hug a tree in broad daylight? You must've seen that I was out of my mind, and on top of that, perhaps I even frightened you.

I don't remember anymore how it began. Slowly, slowly. A little anxiety that grew. Insomnia. Tremors. Sudden panic during a flight. Feeling anxious in the dark enclosure of a movie theater. Headaches, difficulty breathing, frantic checking of pulse and heart rate, dry mouth, pins and needles in my feet. Fear got the better of me. From the fear came a wish to die over the years, a longing to be released from the agony. But also a fear of that same death. An inferno of opposing desires. One day I stopped working. One day I stayed in bed. I stopped answering the phone, I just stopped. I let myself be dismissed from the high school where I was teaching, received unemployment, sick days, and later, social security. And later, much later, the earth, the trees, the rain. Especially the trees. Their certain endurance in this world, *standing*, in the same spot, moving and under the influence of everything around them, but they don't move, they never move until someone cuts them down. And even then, it doesn't necessarily end their lives—it's not easy to get rid of a tree. The stump sprouts and soon it's tall and dense again, growing wildly. I now dedicate my life to a silver maple. No evil can reach me when I crawl up and sit like a monkey in the twisted branches. And this was right where you found me, the next time you happened to see me. This time you came closer. Smiling. Curious.

"Hi."

I nodded a little.

"Why are you sitting up there?"

I stared.

"Aren't you the one that looked so sad last Tuesday, when you were bending over the roses?"

"I'm not sad."

"No?"

I shook my head.

"You look sad."

You made as if to go.

"Wait," my voice strangely woolen. "Wait, wait a minute." I began to climb clumsily down.

Your mouth was wide and soft. You reached your hand out, I took it hesitantly, and you helped me down.

We began to walk. You had that blue hat on, but then you took it off and put it in your pocket. You shook your head so that your hair fell around your face.

"Do you come here often?"

I nodded, "I love to walk under the big trees."

"And to climb them!" you said laughing.

"And to climb them, yes." I tried to smile.

"Last Tuesday," I mumbled. "Last Tuesday you looked very happy."

"Did I?"

"I couldn't forget your face." You looked down. We turned to go up the steps near the rock gardens. A small stream gurgled. I was about to flee. Then you stopped suddenly and laid your hand on my arm. "What's wrong with you?"

"Nothing." Your hand was still resting on my greasy sleeve. "Nothing's wrong with me."

Then something slipped in me. Something raged through me, lava, a storm, everything went black. I invited you for a cup of coffee.

Then you were sitting across from me at the outdoor café in the garden. It was cool, but not cold, heavy clouds sat low over the city, a pair of terribly weakened wasps crawled about in the grass near my feet. I watched their death struggle and almost forgot you, was almost completely absorbed, was almost gone, but then you lifted your cup and asked, "Do you live near here?"

We talked. You had recently moved to the city to study biology. You were majoring in botany. You told me about the plants and flowers, about species and families, about names and soil conditions, about light and shadows, about blooming and seeding, about reproduction and propagation, your cheeks were red, you told me about the trees, you tied your shoelaces, you clutched your mug with both hands, you blew on it, you burned your tongue, you told me your name. Laura. And I, more worn than you, woke up, listened, drank my coffee, lit a cigarette, watched your gesticulating hands, followed your gaze out over the lawn, up to the sky, answered your questions briefly, thought no thoughts, there was only you, right before me, and you shivered, pulled your jacket closer around your body, took your hat out of your pocket again, warmed your hands in it, and then we got up and walked slowly through the garden and out to the street.

I stopped and turned toward you. "Perhaps we'll meet again." You nodded. And then that movement with your hand. I stood there watching you until you turned into the entrance of the university. Warm and cold. The rest of the day I could do nothing else but walk, relying on my steps, needing to stay in motion, and I didn't go home until long after it had gotten dark and I was so exhausted that I fell asleep right on my stomach with my head buried deeply into my stained pillow.

Maybe I had fallen down a crevasse, a sudden slide down an all-too-slippery passageway. Maybe this is it. And in this chrysalis, in this recess, in this hole I've been waiting either for life to notice me again and pull me up, or death to force me down the last few feet and away. I don't eat much. I don't sleep much. Sometimes it's as if I were possessed by a ghost, at other times it's clear to me that I've created this nonexistence that my life has turned into. I didn't meet you the following week. The wind drove hard from the northwest, the leaves rattled down and whirled around on the grass. I washed myself in the kitchen. I rubbed my member with a washcloth. I noticed my sunken stomach, pulled on the loose skin, sighed, and smoked. One Wednesday at the end of October I gave up. The night frost had made the earth hard and cold, I lay on my back behind the ferns, hidden by the bushes, I lay looking up at the drifting clouds and the tops of the trees swaying quietly from side to side. The storm had shaken off the leaves. I was heavy in my heart, limp, and numb. Maybe now. If I lie here long enough. Maybe now it'll end. But an almost tender joy sprung up in me: in that moment I was not afraid of death. Heavy and limp. Ready to give in. Then I heard crunching. Footsteps nearby. And suddenly you were standing over me, looking me in the eye for a second before breaking out in laughter. I got up on my elbows. You shook your head, smiling.

"There *is* something wrong with you!"

I had to get on all fours before standing up. I was stiff from the cold. We stood facing each other. Then your expression became serious.

"Do you know that bracken is very poisonous? It contaminates the ground water, it's carcinogenic." You sounded like a child reading from a book. It was unpleasant, painful to stand so close; I couldn't move my mouth to say anything.

"Come on. I'll get you a cup of coffee. You must be freezing." On the way to the outdoor café you started to laugh again. Then you stopped suddenly, as if you just realized it was inappropriate.

You told me that you often took a walk in the garden during your lunch break, that you're homesick for the fields and forest, and your brothers who still live at home. You were visiting there last weekend. You had helped your mother till the kitchen garden. You chatted, told me about a friend who was an apprentice hairdresser in a salon back home, about how you'd been enemies. Then you became silent. We both sipped our coffee. I stubbed out my cigarette with my foot. You looked at me, staring into my eyes.

"Why do you lie on the ground like that?"

Suddenly I could see how young you were. There was something sulky and innocent in your face, maybe it was the way you pressed your mouth down, maybe because your eyes were so large and clear. But there was also a defiance: the way you continued to hold my gaze.

"Come on. Tell me."

Then I smiled.

"Ah, it's not easy to explain. I think it's good for me. I just like to look up at the trees."

"You and your trees," you said, looking sad.

And then with sudden courage, I got an overwhelming feeling of being an adult and that I should reassure you:

"Take my hand."

You looked frightened, your lips parted as if you wanted to say something, you hesitated, but then you laid your white hand in mine, and I closed it around yours, encircling it, covering it.

We looked at each other, the clouds might have gathered over us because it got darker, a gust of wind blew the paper napkins onto the gravel. I caressed the back of your hand with my finger. And you still looked frightened, though you didn't take your hand away, and I could tell that after awhile you relaxed a little.

"You looked so happy that Tuesday," I said, and almost whispered: "I couldn't forget your face."

The day after, we met again. We nearly bumped into each other when you stepped onto the path near the herb beds. It was a beautiful day. The sun was shining, and the light was soft and at the same time blindingly sharp. We walked down to the pond. The willows were reflecting in the muddy green water. Some coots glided under the bridge. They whistled in the tall reeds. We watched for a while. I thought about how it felt to touch your skin. I didn't dare look at you. I had no idea what to say. You carefully laid your hand on my shoulder and asked if we should go see the tropics.

We stepped into the humid warmth of the greenhouse. You took your hat off and unbuttoned your jacket, and for a long time we stood looking at the carnivorous plants. You said, "That's a pitcher plant. It traps the insects in its sticky funnel." I pushed the heavy flower and it swung back and forth. You laughed. Then you saw a butterfly that was sitting on a fat dark green leaf flapping its wings. Delicate tiny sweat drops appeared on your upper lip. We stood so close that our shoulders touched. Water dripped gently from the palms. I was about to lean against you, but then you walked away and squatted before a twining plant. You studied the underside of one of its leaves. And then looked at me smiling, a look I couldn't decipher. Your eyes threw off sparks. That's how I remember it. When we went outside again the cold was overwhelming. You buttoned up your coat and began to walk. You found a bench in the sun. We sat there for at least ten minutes without saying anything. You leaned back and closed your eyes, and I'm almost certain that you drew a little closer, I could feel your arm pushing against mine. I held my breath, and then suddenly you opened your eyes and got up. You said you had to go, you were late already.

That night I woke up crying, bathed in sweat. I had dreamed that in one single night a hurricane had stripped the leaves off all the trees in the world. I was in despair. Bare black trunks and a trembling stillness. I cried over my loneliness, which I only now understood. And I scolded myself. How could I think that you desired my company? In the mirror I saw a pathetic figure, unshaven, half bald, gray, dull red eyes with an empty expression. I couldn't stop crying. I stayed in bed all the next day. It was Friday, I was weak and warm. I staggered down to buy a few groceries. It wasn't until Tuesday that I returned to the garden. But I was unable to enter my silver maple. It rejected me. Or was it the opposite? The tree was silent. I felt unworthy. That's how I was standing there, limp arms hanging at my sides, staring at the tree, at the yellow and light green leaves at its base, my legs shaking under me, wearing a coat that was far too big, when you walked up behind me, stood there quietly for a little while. I felt your gaze, and then saw you turn around. I saw your back. I saw you hurry away. In no way can I blame you for avoiding me. I would've done the same.

The garden suddenly seemed sinister in that gray light. I realized nothing was blooming anymore. The rosebuds were brown at the edges, diminished and curled up. They'll never unfold. From the covered bench I could see the wide staircase that leads up to the greenhouse. I thought I saw you up there with your hand resting on the railing as if you were on your way down, maybe you'd already put one foot on the first step. I looked away, but when I looked back a second later no one was there.

It got darker, rainier, colder. I was stuck. A panic attack took hold of me. I woke up in the middle of the night with my heart in a wild gallop, terror-stricken, certain that my end was near. I sat at the edge of the bed in the dim light, feverishly checking my pulse, convinced that I *was* dead, that there was no relief, that eternity was *here*, on this planet, in this damp apartment, and I imagined that your last moment alive turns into eternity. The way lightning is materialized in a piece of glass. But then not completely, because I imagined eternity as a living picture—a looping, unending repetition, a prison of arrested time. And soon I began to obsessively think about how I should ensure a means of dying happily, preferably in a state of well-being, empty well-being. Which led me to masturbate every time I was struck by anxiety. Or I tried to. I decided that from the perspective of eternity, the seconds just after an orgasm would be a perfect moment. But all too often I just sat there with my limp member in my hand, out of breath. All too often I cried. And winter came, from my window I could see out over the snow-covered roofs and hear the sound of traffic becoming more and more woolen and distant. I dreamed about your springy step. Your hand drawing a half-circle in the air.

It was well into January before I dared to take a stroll in the garden again. It had snowed a lot. Tiny ice-pearls glittered on the twigs and straw. Some great tits pecked hungrily at frozen paradise apples. A skinny cat ran across the path. The clear air was doing me good. I looked for pebbles in the gravel under the snow. I rattled them around in my hand in my pocket. I was getting closer to my silver maple. It was so beautiful. The sun shone on the thick snow that was covering the branches. I reached out and tentatively caressed the trunk. I rubbed my cheek against the bark. I pressed my lower body against it. Tears welled up in my eyes. And I realized you were gone. I accepted it. It was as if in that moment I became calm and accepted it. Maybe I anticipated a new start for my life. In any case, I was back in the garden by the tree;

relieved, I slid down into the deep snow, ate it, washed my face with it.

But you were not gone. Three weeks later I followed you on the garden paths. A peculiar chase. Filled with energy you moved with self-assurance and determination, while I reeled behind you, hiding behind bushes and trees, sprinting then creeping out of breath behind the red shed when you suddenly stopped and turned to sit on a bench. You pulled a pack of cigarettes out of your purse. You took your gloves off so that I could see your hands. You had painted your nails blue. Then you lifted your face to the sun. Large black sunglasses hid your eyes. It was clear you had changed. I saw how confidently you inhaled the smoke into your lungs with a long drag, how you toyed with a small red phone, and a smile flickered across your face when you apparently received a text. You crossed one leg over the other, you twisted your hair between your fingers and pushed your glasses up on your forehead—and then you looked directly into my eyes. I fought to endure your gaze. You threw the cigarette down and continued to stare at me and I endured it. I did not let go of your eyes and you would not let go of mine. Your look was angry and defiant. Then at last I looked away. My footprints were deep holes in the snow. You got up from the bench and came storming over to me.

I could smell you. Your mouth was painted dark red. A little stone sparkled in your nose. You were very close. First you spoke low, almost tenderly, to me:

"Where have you been? Where have you been all this time?"

I didn't answer. Then more accusingly:

"Where have you been?"

Finally you yelled, your spit hit my face like a spritz of water. "WHERE?!"

"Away," I mumbled.

"What did you say?!"

"I've been away."

"AWAY?!" You kicked at the snow furiously with your foot. Then you stood still with your hands on your hips:

"I thought..." And you took a deep breath.

"What did you think?"

"That we..."

I stared at you for a long time. You were so close.

"I thought that you..." Now you looked unhappy.

I wanted to speak. Then suddenly you sneered at me.

"You're fucking sick in the head!"

I wanted to say something. You came even closer. I could feel your warm breath. You glared at me. Your hair brushed my chin. And then you grabbed my cheeks with your hands and pressed your mouth against mine and stuck your tongue into my mouth and it was fierce and hard. I was shocked. I pulled my head back. You held me tightly. You bit me. You pressed your body against mine. I couldn't breathe. You pinned me against the shed and drove your stiff tongue round and round in my mouth. It was very unpleasant. Then at last you let me go. I was gasping for air. Still low, but not tender: "I wanted to have sex with you in the bathroom. I've thought about it a lot." And then you yelled, "But now it doesn't matter!"

And you shook your head; I was terribly dizzy and bent over. Now more shrilly: "I wanted to make out with you!"

Then you shoved my shoulder hard so that I nearly lost my footing.

"Say something!"

I slowly got up. But I couldn't say anything. I saw your

mouth move, quick and hostile, but I couldn't hear you. Then at last you left. You tripped on a rock. You moved quickly over the white lawn, but then you turned. You stood there a while looking at me. And then, then you made that movement with your hand. And my heart sang. A pile of snow slid down from the roof and landed with a muffled sound next to me. I saw you turn by the linden trees. It occurred to me that maybe you were under the influence, or upset about something. And then again, maybe not. My breath pumped everything out of me. I was freezing. The pale sun was low in the sky, and the sky was white. My heart sang. Your disgusting kiss had postponed death. And your hand had waved me back to life. That's the way it was, there was no doubt about it. The time of waiting was over. Slowly, slowly. I rose up the same way a turtle moves toward the surface of the water.

THE CAR TRIP

Nikolaj slams the car door, and then they realize that Tobias isn't in the car. "God damn it," he says looking at Mia who unfastens her seat belt and gets out. He follows her with his gaze as she walks back to the house, and watches her fumbling with the keys. "When are we going to be there?" asks Signe, and Baby Brother starts to cry. Nikolaj turns and reaches for the pacifier on the floor, but it rolls under the front seat. "Give him the pacifier," he says to Andreas who's engrossed in a comic book. "Give it to him right now!" Andreas grudgingly sticks his hand under the seat and grabs the pacifier. Baby B becomes quiet. Nikolaj watches the house impatiently. Then at last Mia comes, pushing Tobias in front of her. The sulking, lanky fifteen-year-old boy looks straight ahead. Nikolaj senses a rustling, like a gust of wind blowing through reeds, as if the reeds are growing inside him. He clenches his teeth and starts the car. Tobias squeezes into the back seat. Andreas says, "He's sitting on my leg." Signe says, "Ow! Shit!" "Alright," says Mia with a stern, decisive tone, "let's go."

She looks at the children in the backseat as the car pulls out of the driveway. Signe pushes Andreas, Baby B sucks energetically on both his pacifier and his thumb, and Tobias, who's put his hood on, presses his head against the window. "We're going to be late," says Nikolaj. "Why did you take so long?" "My mother called. She's still in the hospital." Mia turns on the radio. "I said we'd stop by on our way home." Nikolaj isn't listening to her. He leans forward to see the road better. It's raining. The windows steam up quickly and they have to open the window a crack even though they're driving on the highway and Mia's neck is getting rained on. She passes out candy. Signe says she's car sick. Andreas says he has to pee. And a little while later: "If you don't stop now, I'm going to pee on the seat."

At the gas station Tobias climbs out and lights a cigarette with his back to the car, bending over his phone. By the time they're ready to go, he's drenched. "Tobias reeks of smoke," says Signe, holding her nose. "And wet dog," says Andreas. "Leave Tobias alone," says Mia, who's in an awkward position with one arm reaching into the backseat to give Baby B a bottle. "Can't Signe do it?" asks Nikolaj. "I don't want to," Signe answers. "It's not about wanting to," says Nikolaj, and Mia says, "It's all right. I can do it." The rain is really coming down now. Big trucks pass them, spraying their windshield with dirty water. "We'll never make that ferry." Nikolaj is chomping anxiously on a piece of nicotine gum. "Let's see," says Mia. At last, Baby B falls asleep. Mia watches his pale face and the blood vessels that tint his eyelids blue. She rubs her aching arm and hand. Tobias's phone is constantly making noises. "How come Tobias gets to use his phone in the car and I'm not allowed to?" Signe kicks Nikolaj's backseat rhythmically. "Why aren't you answering me?" "Stop kicking your father's seat," says Mia. "If he can then I can, too," says Signe, taking her phone out. Intolerable noises from Signe's phone mix with noises from Tobias's. "Stop KICKING, Signe," Nikolaj says.

"Put your phone away," says Mia. But Signe, who has now stopped kicking continues to play different ringtones. "You're going to wake up Baby B," says Mia, turning around so she can grab Signe's phone. Laughing, Signe lifts it up so she can't reach it. Mia loosens her seatbelt and twists her body around, she's practically on her knees, pressing herself between the two front seats. "I can't see shit when you're sitting like that," says Nikolaj. Mia grabs Signe's arm and wrestles the phone away from her. "Ow! Ow, shit, my fucking arm!" "Watch your mouth." Mia is sweating. Signe pretends she's crying. The baby wakes up with a scream. Mia lifts her hand as if she's going to give Signe a hard slap on the head. "Look what you've done! Give him the pacifier, Andreas." Andreas gives Baby B the pacifier and pats him mechanically on the cheek as he continues reading the comic book. "I want that comic book, it's my turn," whines Signe with a tearful voice. "Mom said we had to share it." "Leave your brothers alone, Signe," says Mia. "I'm not doing anything! You said yourself we had to share it!" She's becoming hysterical. Mia gives her a candy. Then it becomes quiet in the backseat, the only sound is Baby B's wheezing inhalations. "I hope he's not getting sick," Mia says to Nikolaj. "He was coughing so much last night." Nikolaj doesn't answer. She notices how his jaw works when he chews. Mia presses her cheek against the cold damp window. She listens to the windshield wipers and drifts off a bit. Dreamlike thoughts dart around like restless insects. There's something with Nikolaj's hand sliding up in her. Her own mouth that's sucking on his fingers. A bird landing in a treetop. And there are dark images of herself moving down a long corridor where doors on both sides are banging open, but there's no one else there, only these empty offices that open when she walks by and the sound of her shoes hitting the shiny floor. "Are you sleeping?" asks

Nikolaj. "No, no." "I don't think he's getting sick," says Nikolaj. And after a brief pause: "When we get there we should make a plan." "A plan?" "For how we want the vacation to go." "What do you mean?" "It's important that we lay down some rules." "What?" "For the kids." Nikolaj glances at her. "Yeah, which chores we want them to do, how far they can go alone, and when they need to be home by." She watches Nikolaj's profile, and reaches over to touch his hair. He glances at her again. She smiles at him. He puts his hand in her lap, and she puts her hands over his. "Tobias is going to babysit once in awhile so we can have some time to ourselves," he says in a low voice. "No way," says Tobias. "I'm leaving on Friday. Niki's getting back from her vacation, and there's no way I'm going to rot in that summerhouse." "Tobias," says Mia, "we've already talked about this, now stop it. Niki's welcome to join us." Tobias shakes his head under his hood. He stares at her coldly in the rearview mirror until Mia slides over to the side so that she's out of his view. "That's what I'm talking about," says Nikolaj. "We need to make clear agreements." "But we've already done that," says Mia. "I want that comic book now. That's what we agreed on," shouts Signe, who has apparently finished eating her candy, judging from her long silence. She rips the magazine out of Andreas's hand and begins kicking the front seat. "I'm hungry," says Andreas. "I'll die of starvation if you don't stop now."

They can see the ship far out at sea when they drive down to the ferry landing. The rain is letting up, and there's one hour before the next boat leaves. "We should've taken the bridge, that's what I said," says Nikolaj. "How much money do we get for candy?" asks Signe. "You said we were going to get money for candy." Mia gets out. Signe pulls on her coat. "Give us the money!" Nikolaj heads for the bathrooms, and Andreas is nowhere to be found. Mia looks down the long row of cars. She looks over at the waiting room where Nikolaj just opened the door and is walking in. "Where's Andreas?" Tobias shrugs his shoulders. She looks toward the sea. "Where IS he?" She calls out. She yells his name. She runs past the cars. She goes all the way over to the first car in line and then runs to the gangplank connecting the harbor to the ferry. Andreas isn't there either. She hears the waves hitting hard against the pier and stops, out of breath, to look up and down the coast. There's no sign of his green windbreaker, or his blonde hair. She now imagines the boy dead, the funeral, her own derangement, and she even starts to imagine how she'll lose interest in the other children if Andreas is gone. She'll lose interest in Nikolaj, and won't be able to live with him or anyone else. The wind rips through her coat and blows her hair in her face. Suddenly a red burning hate for all of them surges through her, then she breaks down and starts crying uncontrollably with strange, ugly sounds that are quickly carried away by the wind. Then she can't breathe in between the wails, as if the wind is preventing it, and she becomes overwhelmed by an even greater and terrifying anxiety for her own life, her own death. That's how she's standing there, swaying with her coat flapping, one hand on her mouth, her eyes wet and wild, when Tobias appears, walking toward her at a very slow pace. He has his hands in his pockets, his hood tied around his face, and the wind fills his oversized pants with air. He looks ridiculous. He stands next to her. Mia is overcome by a new fit of crying. She tries to say Andreas's name but all that comes out of her mouth is sobs. "Calm down. They found him." She takes her hand away from her mouth. "Where?!" she screams. "Who knows. He went down to look at some car." "A car?!" she screams. Tobias gives her a look of contempt. "Yeah. A car." He pulls his shoulders up and lets them fall, then he turns and begins to walk away from her at the same slow pace as before, back toward the endless row of cars. One last time, Mia looks out across the water. She sighs deeply and rubs her eyes. Then she staggers back after him.

Andreas is sitting in the backseat reading his comic book. He doesn't react to Mia's outburst of fury and affection, he turns away when she tries to hold his face, he pulls his arm back when she searches for his hand. Signe is sitting next to him stuffing herself with candy. Nikolaj has taken Baby B out of the car seat and now he's bent over Nikolaj's arm, in that heavy snowsuit that makes his body look stuffed and deformed. His arms stick out helplessly, and he babbles with delight when he sees Mia, snot bubbles blowing out his nose. Nikolaj looks at her with a puzzled, tender expression. "Were you crying?" he asks. She sticks her hand into Tobias's pocket and pulls out his cigarettes. "What the hell are you doing?" says Tobias. She turns her back to the wind and lights it. Nikolaj furrows his brow and takes a step back. "Mom! What are you doing?" Tobias rips the cigarette pack out of her hand. "Mia, what the hell…" says Nikolaj. "We agreed we weren't going to smoke." Mia walks over to the waiting room. He shouts after her, "You quit smoking, Mia!" She pulls the door open and sits on a bench. It smells of old, cold smoke. Two young girls are giggling sharing a cigarette. Mia smokes intensely until she becomes nauseated. Then she goes to the bathroom and drinks some water from the tap. In the mirror, her face is puffy from crying, her mascara and eye shadow run down her cheeks, it looks like someone has rubbed ashes all over her face.

Nikolaj has already started the car when she gets back. The children are sitting in their seats. Signe has given Baby B a lollipop, and clearly one of them has farted because it smells like a rotten egg. Mia rolls down her window. No one says a word. Nikolaj looks inquiringly at her, and Mia thinks: All is lost. His face looks sad. He looks as if he's undone. She puts her hand on his knee. "I'm sorry," she says, even though that wasn't what she wanted to say. "You owe me a cigarette," Tobias says. Signe starts singing the same two lines of a song over and over, and Andreas kicks her in the shin, Baby B grabs Signe's hair and tries to stick it in his sticky mouth that the lollipop has dyed bright green. Andreas and Signe burst out laughing over Baby B's green mug. They can't stop pointing and shrieking, even Tobias can't hold back a smile.

On the ferry, Andreas and Signe get some money to play the slot machine and, in return, they have to take Baby B to the playroom when they're done. Tobias disappears with a can of coke and his phone. Mia feeds the baby applesauce from a jar and Nikolaj goes to get coffee. The ferry rocks. After the older children take Baby B, Nikolaj sits down next to Mia. He puts his arm around her and pulls her close to him. "Sweetheart," he says. And they sit like that for a little while, silent, with the steaming coffee in front of them, watching the crowd of people around them. "What was that about your mother?" asks Nikolaj. "How is she? Better?" Mia nods. The coffee sloshes around in her stomach every time the ferry leans to the side. She's hungry. Nikolaj looks like he wants to say something else, but suddenly Signe appears with Baby B in her arms. "He pooped in his pants," she says. "He stinks like shit." Nikolaj takes the stinky child. She hands him a diaper. She notices how he smiles to Baby B as he walks away, kissing him and saying something in his ear. At first when Tobias sits down at the table she doesn't recognize him. It's not until he says something to her that she realizes it's him. "I'm going home on Friday, Mom. There's a party at Johannes's, and anyway, Niki's coming home." He's sitting across from her with both hands flat on the table, leaning forward, and looking her right in the eye. "I'm going whether you give me permission or not. Just so you know. I can stay at Dad's house." "He's in London." "I have a key." Mia shakes her head, thinking that it'll end up with her letting him go, having no idea if it's the right thing to do. Tobias gets up abruptly and goes off. It's as if a gust of wind is blowing through the reeds, and the reeds are growing inside her; she holds her breath. Nikolaj comes back and puts Baby B on her lap. "Tobias is going back on Friday," she says. "That's exactly what I was saying," says Nikolaj. "We should've just let him stay home." "But didn't you say you wanted him to watch the kids at the summerhouse?" Baby B sticks his hand in her mouth, digging into her lips with his small sharp nails. "As long as he's here, he can just as well help out. Don't you think?" Mia looks down at the table. Violent hunger, her stomach rumbles. "Honey," says Nikolaj, removing Baby B's hand from her mouth. "It's a good arrangement, don't you think? He's with us a few days, and then he goes home. Everyone gets what they want." Mia looks up, he pushes a lock of hair away from her cheek and tucks it behind her ear. He puts his hand on the back of her neck. Then all of a sudden, he kisses her, his tongue gliding over her teeth, the blood rushes between her legs, she grabs his hair, and Baby B whimpers, he's getting squished between their bodies as they try to get closer. At that moment, she recognizes Andreas's loud crying, he's sprained his left foot jumping off the slide in the playroom and landing wrong.

The car is full of candy wrappers, toys, and empty Coke cans. Tobias is now sitting in the front, and Mia has squeezed herself into the backseat with the children. She sings for Baby B. Signe sings along. Andreas sits between them, pale and silent. Mia strokes his hair. After awhile, Nikolaj and Tobias begin talking. She hears snippets of their conversation in the pauses between the children's songs, something about a rally that apparently Tobias has been to, something about the EU soccer championship, something about the number of absences Nikolaj had in German class when he was in high school. It's clearing up, but the sky is still dark in some places, dark gray, dark blue, and deep purple. Mia sings looking out the window. Wet plough marks, and now and then a strip of forest. The road winds through the hilly landscape. She remembers sitting on the bench freezing when she was on vacation at her aunt's house. She can distinctly feel the goose bumps on her arms, her hair that tasted like snot, and in front of her, there's a Nutella sandwich with flies landing on it. She's sitting at a table with a plastic tablecloth, to the right of the cupboard, on that smooth wooden bench, and she pinches herself on the knees and spreads Nutella around on the plate. She sniffs and sucks on her hair, the flies tickle her bare feet, she kicks at them, and in the background the radio is playing in the kitchen, pots clatter in the sink. And all the while there's a terror inside her, which her aunt calls homesickness, a very physical longing for her mother's body: to lean against her legs wrapped in nylon stockings and her hard hip, to reach out and grab hold of her. And mother's breath is often sour, but she lets her mother breathe on her anyway without turning away, even though it's so unpleasant, she sits there anyway, close to her large angular body, while she picks at a little sore near mother's mouth, that's it, that's the way it should be, and now her aunt comes into the room, puts her hands on her hips, and asks if she's really still sitting there playing with her food. Mia slides back and forth between the child's body on the bench and herself sitting here in the crowded car, where she can't even move, her wet feet in rubber boots, squeezing Baby B's pacifier in her hand. And it's not until Signe shouts, "Mom! Are you even listening to me?" that she opens her hand, allowing the pacifier to fall to the floor of the car, and she stares into Signes's outraged face, "Holy shit, Mom, you're so weird. Are you sleeping or what?" "Watch your mouth," she says sternly. Nikolaj smiles at her in the rearview mirror, she smiles stiffly back.

They stop at a cafeteria in a small town about twenty miles from the summerhouse. Andreas limps and needs help getting up the stairs. Signe bursts out and begins to run around and around on the lawn, shrieking with delight. Nikolaj and Tobias get the food, and Mia tries to give Baby B his milk, but he can't concentrate on sucking. When they sit down to eat, Nikolaj slides his hand up under her blouse, and she fumbles for his cock under the table. They look at each other. His eyes are blurry, a strong desire rises in her, and he tries to stick his hand down her pants. Then Baby B lets out a cry and hurls himself back in his high chair. He shrieks so loudly that people around them are shocked and turn their heads to see what's going on, and she gets up, lifts him, and goes outside. He gasps for breath between his earsplitting cries. He flails about wildly. She walks back and forth in front of the cafeteria, rocking him and speaking to him in a soothing voice, but nothing helps. Nikolaj comes out with the bottle, and now they're both standing there in their thin shirts chilled to the bone as they try to get him to take the bottle. The milk goes down the wrong way and he starts coughing. It looks like he's choking to death. Mia shakes him. Then he begins to cry again, furious, and with renewed energy. Mia catches sight of the children still sitting at the table in the cafeteria. It looks like Signe and Andreas are fighting over some french fries. Signe hits Andreas on the head. Andreas pulls her ponytail. They tumble to the floor. A man at a nearby table gets up to intervene, while his wife sits there shaking her head in disgust. Nikolaj runs to the car with the screaming baby, and Mia runs up the steps into the cafeteria. The children are still on the floor. Signe is sobbing. Andreas licks ketchup off his fingers. The couple at the next table watch her as she gathers the coats and bags, yells to Tobias, who can't hear her because of the music blasting in his ears, that they're leaving. She grabs Signe and Andreas and hustles them out. Andreas whines, "Why are we leaving already? I haven't finished eating." "God, take it easy!" yells Signe, jerking her hand free, "I haven't done anything! What have I done?"

Baby B doesn't calm down until ten minutes after they've been driving, and Signe and Andreas hold their hands over their ears and stare accusingly at Mia as he screams his head off. She has a bland taste of fat and weak coffee in her mouth. It's going to be dark soon. She thinks about how she's looking forward to lying close to Nikolaj's body. How nice it'll be to get there, and how they'll all have a good vacation after all. She thinks that they'll have to get a doctor to look at Andreas's foot. She looks down at her white folded hands. And she feels her heart skip a beat when she lifts her hand and puts it on Tobias's shoulder. She gives it a squeeze, he turns halfway and looks at her confused with his dark eyes. That's when her phone rings. A voice says it's about her mother. She's dead.

CONFERENCE

It's strange to meet you here, after so many years, and to still feel disturbed just being near your body. The way you're *settled* in the chair like a big contented animal, like a large wild cat licking itself in the sun, or an elephant bathing in a river, like a person resting on top of another after pleasurable sex, it has an intimidating and shameless effect on me. My complete attention turns toward you and I'm unable to relax. It's as if I am overflowing my banks.

The rhythm of my heart became irregular. I froze. I sweated. I was unable to control my facial expressions. A thin man, who kept taking off and putting on his glasses, lectured, apparently about economic growth in the Far East. You were sprawled in the armchair in front of me and I could see the nape of your neck, the light skin of your throat, your strangely rounded thighs pressing against the black fabric of your pants, and your thick wide hands relaxed in your lap. I could see your breathing in your back, how it blew you up a bit, how your shoulder blades slid away from each other a little before coming together again. And the whole time I saw you in front of me naked. It frightened me, like a kind of obsession, something inevitable: a clear image of your whole body standing in my bedroom, a smile slowly spreading across your face and then your head sliding back at an angle, really enjoying it, while your red and blue prick shines wildly between your legs. The whole time I saw you naked, sitting in that armchair in front of me reflected in the mirror hanging on the wall in front of you, when I saw you smile at something someone said, or when I saw you close your eyes, pressing them shut in an odd grimace. That's also disturbing: the way you take up so much space; the way you always make those grimaces whenever you're with complete strangers. But I'm no stranger. And I am a stranger. It's been so many years that we've definitely become strangers to each other, but we'll never be complete strangers to each other. That's what makes it so unbearable. It made me sick just looking at you, and yet I can't look away. Then you slide your hand up and rest it on the back of your neck, lightly supporting your large head, completely relaxed. You turn your face so that I can see your nose, a little of one eye, half your mouth, the wrinkled but surprisingly moist skin over your jaw. And in the mirror on the wall I see the other side of your face, where the skin of your jaw is tight and smooth because you're turning your head slightly to the other side. Perhaps someone has said something funny. Because now you laugh out loud, hoarse and unabashed, your mouth opening, and even your teeth I know, every one of them, the wet gums, and the brown discoloration at the back of your bottom teeth. I'm shocked. Your laughter shocks me. It feels like an animal has snuck up on me and suddenly it's close, ready to attack. I accidentally utter a peculiar sound from deep within my throat. I adjust myself in the chair, pressing my hands between my thighs. You've thrown your leg up over the armrest, and now you swing your foot and shin rhythmically back and forth. Your shoes are black and shiny. I can see your socks. The leg is swinging. Your hand leaves the neck and reaches for the coffee cup on the table in front of you. Your lips purse together as if to kiss and slurp from the cup. You bend forward, putting it down again. Loudly you clear your throat. A muscle begins to twitch just above my knee in a painless spasm. And now I suddenly notice how cold my feet are, almost numb, at least the toes are, way down in my thin boots. And now I notice how warm my face is, it must be red and blotchy, there's throbbing behind my eyes, and my mouth is dry. When there's a break a little while later, I get up carefully, noticing how stiff my legs are when I walk the few yards to the table with water. I spill some as I pour it. Your gaze on my back. No doubt unintentional. I stumble out of the room and sit on the toilet breathing fast for a long time.

During lunch you come over to me and ask a few simple questions. It's been a long time. How've you been? Your gaze searches in all directions as if you were dreaming with your eyes open. I hear myself answer. I pour some whole milk in my glass. You say something else and laugh. You lay your hand on my shoulder and give a little pull before going over to your seat at the other table. I drink all the milk. It stings where you had placed your hand. As if you had made an imprint on my skin. And that's exactly what you've done. Like no one else you have made an imprint on my skin. I'm covered in scars. I'm not ungrateful to you. It's one of my life's great experiences. It's hard to explain. It's chemistry. And I remember it as a situation without willpower, which was certainly so full of will. For your flesh. Back then. The white cloth of the sheet clenched in my fist. Your hand lifting the cigarette to your mouth. The sound of water sliding down your throat. My own wide-open eyes. The skin on my back. When you bend over it. And this scent from you hanging in the air even though you're now sitting several yards away eating quickly with concentration, quite civilized, but with a hidden, unruly greediness: the scent of dry tobacco before it's rolled into cigarettes, the scent of perfume that's nearly washed off, the scent of booze digested long ago, ecstasy that burned out long ago, and all that's left is a little prickling nausea. That scent. Which I was drawn into. Which I adore. But not without resistance. Because I know so well that you bring imbalance. I know this deep within my body. Just like I know that I can't tolerate milk. And that's what made me so desperate and angry. There's only you. And I vanished. It's physics. It's like a tree that moans when the branches rub against each other but they can't move away. One of them wears out and it falls down, only to decay on the ground. It's physics that determines which branch must surrender. I fell long and hard. Now you put the fork and knife down and suppress a burp. I glide my tongue over the slimy membrane the milk has left in my mouth. My hand lies heavy and relaxed on the table. You bend toward the woman next to you and say something to her. She smiles, confused, and looks at you with large eyes. I have a violent desire to cough. I fall long and hard, a gorge has opened in me down through the throat, rib cage, stomach, I tumble with the racing blood and see my entrails sweeping by. I come to the sizzling stomach and it whirls around in a maelstrom. Dissolving acid around and around. My eyes wide open. The hand squeezing the white cloth. I will shout something hurtful and inappropriate at you. And then I feel at last I can cough. But it turns out that I throw up. I straight out throw up. All over the table and myself, it must've been the milk. I hear a loud ringing in my ears, and then I breathe in with a wheezing whistling sound. Then it gets completely still. You wipe your mouth with your napkin and turn your head slowly slowly to look at me.

INTERRUPTION

When the doorbell rang in the middle of the day—it was a Wednesday, it was drizzling, he was listening to the radio and was about to start reading—he felt strongly that he was being interrupted with something important. It rang again. He got up, irritated, opened the door, and a woman forced her way into his apartment. She shoved him aside with a lot of force and before he knew what was happening she was in his living room, where, out of breath, she dropped down on the corner of the couch and began crying loudly in distress. He'd never seen her before. She looked like she might be from Thailand or maybe the Philippines. At first he spoke kindly to her, asking her what she wanted, what the matter was. When she didn't respond he took her carefully by the shoulders and tried to pull her up. She slapped his face, yelled something incomprehensible, and wailed as if in great pain. He stepped back in shock. And then grabbed her again, this time by the arm, harder, with more anger than shock; she gasped when he pulled. She bit his thumb. He grabbed her hair and pushed her to the floor. She flailed her arms and legs, he lay on top of her, she tried to stick her fingers in his eyes. She kneed him in the groin. He doubled over and let go of her hair and she crept back to the couch, where she again broke down and cried, now more like moaning and whining. He went into the kitchen. Down in the alley the super was sweeping. The pretty red-haired downstairs neighbor came up from the basement laundry room and stuffed a bulging garbage bag into the trash can. He closed the window. His fingertips tingled. It had become quiet in the living room. He stood in the doorway and watched her. His temple pulsed and it felt like everything was swelling up inside him. She had neither socks nor shoes on. She was slumped over and her eyes were closed. He thought she was sleeping and approached her carefully, wanting to get her out. She jumped up and pointed to the window. He followed her gaze. A fat blonde woman stood there looking up and down the street and then headed downstairs to the entrance of the basement and slammed the door shut. The woman gave him a confused look. "Bad woman!" she yelled, tapping on the window with her index finger. He resisted the sudden urge to grab her by the neck and squeeze hard by taking a deep breath. Then she flung her arms around *his* neck. She smelled of cheap perfume and sweat. He blocked his nose and tried to push her away. But she held on tightly. "Please help," she whispered, "please help, big problem." He went slack, feeling almost listless. Then she let her head rest on his chest a moment. She sat down. Her jaw fell open. Her teeth looked as if they had been flung into her mouth. Her feet were unusually small. She scrunched up her toes, as though she were going to pick up a pencil off the floor. "I go home," she then said, staring in his eyes. "Yes," he replied and sunk heavily onto the other end of the couch, "get the fuck out of here." But she didn't move. "Go home," he said, nodding toward the door. She lay down. He could hear her breathing. Her shin brushed against his. A heavy truck drove by rattling the windows. Then he was unsure, maybe it was a bus.

He went back to his books. He turned off the radio. He looked over his notes. He got up again and drank a glass of water. Headache. His eyes wanted to close. He felt dead tired. He looked over at the couch, and there she lay motionless on one side sleeping. He went in the bedroom, which was quiet and cool. He lay on the bed, but was unable to relax.

Some time later he lay down on the bare wood floor. When he woke up he could hear banging in the kitchen. His back was stiff. The woman was in the middle of doing the dishes. Some water was heating in a pot. She gave him a big smile. He noticed that she had washed the floor and hung up clean dish towels. "Very nice," she said, and nodded and smiled again. He shook his head in defeat. Then he pulled himself together, and with determination nudged her toward the hall. She didn't say anything, but it was almost impossible to budge her. He didn't get it, she was so small, he used all his might, and still there was an incomprehensible resistance from her; he huffed and puffed. When he at last got the front door open, she clung to the doorframe, and as he struggled to pry her hands loose, his upstairs neighbor, a real hefty guy, came down the stairs, and she began shouting. He couldn't see any other way out, so he pulled her back inside and shut the door. She went right back into the kitchen and continued doing the dishes. He stood by the window. His stomach felt like a huge trembling hole. A stout bald man came up from the basement in the building across the street. He scratched his groin and unlocked his bike.

The hole in his stomach now felt like hunger. He grabbed his jacket and went to buy some groceries. When he returned, she clapped and shrieked with joy; she took all the food out of the bag and started to cook dinner.

Later in the evening he went out and got a good chunk of weed. He sat down on a bench by the lake and smoked. He went over what he would say if he called the police. He wondered if he could ask someone to help him get rid of her. The thoughts drifted away just as they arose. One duck swam around in the middle of the lake. The rain had stopped, the cloudless sky was bluish-green and light. When he got back, she was lying on the couch watching TV. She didn't look up when he walked into the living room, and he didn't say a word. He locked the bedroom door behind him, spread out on the bed, and immediately fell into a deep sleep.

The next morning he had completely forgotten about her. The curtains fluttered a little. He had dreamed about the redhead—that he was fiddling with her ears—and he had felt calm and relaxed. He went into the living room to find his cigarettes. There she stood with one leg flung up on a chair. She was slathering herself with his moisturizer, and one of his towels, clearly wet, lay on a chair. "Good morning, sir," she said with a huge smile. Her stomach was thick and she had short legs. A long scar twisted up from her pussy and continued past her navel. He went into the bathroom to brush his teeth. The toothbrush was wet. He made do with rinsing his mouth. When he went to make coffee, he burned himself on the pot. It was full. She came running in with a wet cloth for his hurt hand and poured him a cup. She had also cooked rice and some egg concoction that had a smell that nauseated him, but she on the other hand was hungry. "You buy good curry, I make good food," she said, nudging him. Then she laughed out loud. He went right up to her. "Listen," he said intently, "today you will go home. I don't want you here, do you understand? You have to go home." "No, no," was the only thing she said. A glimmer of a smile flashed in her eyes and disappeared again. "No, no, no."

It felt like ants were crawling in his veins. He had a hard time breathing. Down in the street the super was sweeping.

He crossed the street and tried to look in through the tinted window in the basement. A "Closed" sign was hanging on the door.

He met with some of his fellow students to compare notes, and as usual he was quiet, chain smoking; a great uneasiness paradoxically made him sit motionless, locked in the same position. He had to go to the bathroom but didn't get up. On the way home after they were finished, Claes caught up with him. He heard him say something, but it wasn't until Claes grabbed him and looked directly into his eyes that he understood what he had said. "What's the matter with you, are you sick?" he said. "Are you sick?" But he couldn't get any words out. He couldn't say a foreign woman had moved into his apartment against his will. It sounded completely ridiculous. So instead he mumbled that he had stayed up reading most of the night. Claes kept staring at him. "You *are* sick," he said smiling.

When he got home, she was washing his clothes in the kitchen sink. She worked like mad. The clothes that she had already wrung out were hanging here and there from the furniture dripping. He saw that she had washed all the windows. And she'd put on a pair of his socks that were way too big. He came close to picking up a chair and smashing it right in front of her face.

He bought curry. She was a pretty good cook. He taught her how to use the washing machine in the basement. He got her to be quiet while he was reading. But he still couldn't concentrate. He got a blanket from the attic so that she had something to cover herself with at night. She cut her hair with the kitchen scissors. One morning he saw her grooming her pubic hair with his razor. And it was not until one Friday evening when Claes and Jakob dropped by unannounced and quite drunk, a complete surprise because they had never done that before, to see if he wanted to go out drinking, that it became really complicated. "You fucking better come out for a beer with us, you nerd." "Hallo!" she chirped, waving the dish towel. He grabbed his jacket, and hustled them out. She followed them into the hallway and watched with sad dewy eyes. Then suddenly she turned on her heels and closed the door behind her. They stared at him mystified. "What's going on? You have a girlfriend?" Down at the local bar, after they had ordered beer and were sitting at a table, Jakob said, "I didn't know you liked foreign pussy," and then Claes sprayed beer out of his mouth at him, and they both lay over the table, screaming with laughter. He laughed with them. They ordered more beer. A couple of young women sat down next to them. He thought about the red-haired neighbor. One of the women pressed her thigh against his under the table. When Claes and Jakob got really drunk, a fit of vulgarity came over them. But then he also got drunk. "She could be my mother," he yelled, "but I sure as hell don't want to suck those sagging foreign tits!" The two women looked at him horror-struck. He saw himself clenching his fist and hammering down on the table so that glasses and bottles tipped over.

She was lying on the sofa sleeping when he got home. He could see her back and the top of her crack.

Late one afternoon he almost collided with the fat blonde across the street when she came stomping up from the basement. She hissed at him, "Watch out, idiot." Then disappeared down into the depths again. He knocked on the door. Immediately, he had second thoughts and was already on his way up when the door opened. A young Thai woman with many clips in her hair stood in the doorway. "Come, come," she said, motioning with her hand. He didn't move. Another woman came up from behind to see. They said something to each other and began to giggle. "No afraid, come, come," the one with the clips said. Now he could just make out the fat blonde in the dark. She was taking groceries out of the bags. When she saw him she came right over. She shoved the others aside. "Do you want some or not?" He shook his head and hurried away. "You better learn how to make up your mind," she yelled after him. He was already a ways out in the street. "We can't run to the door day and night!" He walked around the block before he went home. He met the super on the stairs, who smiled suggestively. "Well," he said, "they're a bunch of really sweet girls, huh?" He leaned forward. "And talented." Now he was right up against his ear with his smacking lips: "And you can get it from them for hardly anything." He shoved the super aside and stumbled up the stairs. The super yelled after him, "It's nothing to be ashamed of!"

He smoked one joint after another, but he still wasn't able to calm down. The woman sat in the kitchen playing solitaire. She was wearing his bathrobe.

He visited his parents. His mother had made pea soup. They sat in the dining room. His mother told him about his cousin who had probably had a child. His father cleared his throat several times. Through the open door to the garden, he caught a glimpse of his old swing moving ever so slightly in the plum tree. He said nothing about the woman back home. Then the cat came into the room and rubbed against his leg. His parents watched him silently, as if they expected something from him, but he couldn't figure out what it might be. The cat purred delightedly, and in some way it was embarrassing, the animal's open enjoyment, the golden sunshine hitting its fur. When he got back home the woman was sitting on the windowsill staring down at the street. One of her legs swung in the air. The kitchen was a mess. He ordered her testily to clean up. She obeyed with a sigh. He saw the girl with the clips put a piece of cake on a paper plate and a glass with orange liquid out on the sidewalk. She closed her eyes and raised her face toward the evening sun. It looked as if she smiled, but he wasn't sure. He closed the curtain and took a joint from the desk drawer. He lay down on the couch and put on the TV. When she was finished in the kitchen she sat down next to him and lifted his head onto her lap. She caressed his hair with mechanical movements, and he let her do it.

He met the redhead on the bus. He tried to hide, but when they were both about to get off, she noticed him and said hi, and a little while later when he was waiting at a red light, she came up next to him, said hi again, and when he felt pressed to look up, she asked if he had gotten a roommate; she had met the woman in the laundry room. He shook his head. But she continued: "Is she your girlfriend?"

"No."

"Then what?"

"It's my cousin."

"Your cousin?"

"My second cousin."

"But she doesn't speak Danish?" He took a deep breath.

"My uncle and aunt live in Malaysia."

"In Malaysia?"

"Yeah."

The light turned, they began to walk, he picked up his pace, but she caught up. "She seemed sweet. How long is she staying?" He caught her glance and noticed that her eyes were gray, he had always thought they were brown. "Not so long," he mumbled. Then she stopped asking questions, they walked in silence, after awhile she lagged behind. He turned the corner, and when he passed the basement stairs across the street, the four paper plates with cake and candy were still there on the sidewalk. She noticed that he had slowed down and she stopped and said, "It's an offering. Those people must be Buddhist."

"Who?" he asked with a strong desire for her to say out loud what was going on in the basement. "The girls," she answered, "haven't you noticed them?" He shook his head, cut across the street, and unlocked the door. She slipped in with him. Loud music boomed in the entryway, and as they went up the stairs it became clear to him that the music was coming from his apartment. She found her keys in her bag. Then suddenly she turned toward him and looked him in the eye while she listened carefully for a moment, and then came her intimate, restrained, inquisitive question: "Is that your cousin's music?" He hurried up to his apartment. She had wound his wool scarf around her breasts and a towel around her waist. She danced barefoot and wildly around the apartment. The music was earsplitting. The room smelled strongly of sweat. There was an empty bottle of rum on the table. She shrieked, yelled, jumped up and down, stamped, howled, swung her arms round and round. Her eyes were red. He turned down the music. She jumped up on his back and beat him with small weak fists, while bawling drunkenly. "Music, music! Idiot!" Her voice rose up to higher octaves, now in her own language, which he couldn't identify. He grabbed hold of her and carried her into the bathroom. She grunted and became heavy. He put her in the shower and turned on the cold water. She tried to stand, but slipped, she cursed and threatened him. And it sounded as if she had swallowed her own howl as the water gushed down over her. He left the room closing the door. An hour later, she still hadn't come out; it turned out that she was sleeping on the floor. On her back with her thin legs parted. She snored. He could see right up her red, shiny cunt.

He sat at the kitchen table eating pizza, lost in thought about how a big coffee spill made the past week's notes illegible. But there were no thoughts. He lifted the papers up and let them float down to the floor. Then she came slinking in. She crawled under the table, pulled off his socks and began massaging the soles of his feet. She took every single toe into her mouth and sucked on them. He looked up and stared ahead. She let go of the toes with a slurping sound and began pressing and squeezing. When she was finished she came out from under the table and stood smiling broadly at him, then stuck a finger inside her cheek, tilted her head, and went to put on a kettle of water. She suddenly laughed to herself as though she'd just thought of something very amusing. It was tremendously hot in his feet and legs; he'd never experienced such a burning sensation in his body before. He opened the drawer and lit a joint. Slowly he pushed the drawer closed with the palm of his hand, while saying, "If you're still here tomorrow morning I'll call the police." She looked at him provocatively with her chin raised. She didn't say a word. She continued to watch him while he smoked, she stood there completely still with the teapot in one hand, and a white cloud of steam rose up from the pot, slowly pulsing in the air. He went into the bathroom to study his face in the mirror. He looked up his nose. He let his hand glide over his chin. Then he took a cup from the kitchen and headed out. She sat at the kitchen table drinking tea. She still had the wet towel around her waist.

He knocked tentatively on the downstairs neighbor's door. Two pearls glowed on her earlobes. Now her eyes looked blue. He asked if he could borrow some sugar. When she disappeared with the cup, he stepped a little into the entryway and from there could see that she had a whole bunch of green plants both on the windowsills and floor. He thought he heard a bird chirping in there, maybe it was just his imagination. "Say hi to your cousin!" She smiled. On the way downstairs he poured the sugar into the left pocket of his jacket.

She didn't leave. She lay on the couch and watched TV all day. Neither of them said anything. He felt inspired. In the evening he called Claes, who was probably unpleasantly surprised and didn't know what to say. He invited Claes out for a beer and said there was something he wanted to talk to him about. Claes hesitated. But he didn't care, he pushed and persuaded, it was important, he said, and in the end, the defeated Claes reluctantly agreed. It was warm out, a fine green summer light hung in the air until late evening. He touched the sugar in his pocket, letting it sift between his fingers, then collected it in a fist, opened his hand, and licked it off his fingers. The sugar melted on his tongue. Claes looked shy and uneasy about the whole thing. They had never been alone like this before. He told Claes that he had serious problems with a couple of women. They both wanted him and sought him day and night.

They were clearly obsessed with him. He was at the end of his rope. He spoke loudly and with confidence. At first, Claes stared incredulously at him. Then he gasped in amazement and leaned forward. "But. But, do *you* want *them*?" he asked impressed, almost in awe.

"No. Not really."

"But, are they *hot*?"

"I guess so."

Claes grinned widely. His face softened. "What if I just take them off your hands?" A warmth like when she had massaged his feet spread over him. Now that he knew he was so sought after, Claes had clearly changed his view of him. He sensed the new respect, and it was easy for him to take it on: even the way he lit his cigarette was different now, with far more elegance and experience; he leaned back in the chair and slowly lifted the lighter, while Claes followed his movements with an almost voracious gaze.

He threw the keys down on the kitchen counter and looked into the living room. She wasn't lying on the couch. He turned on the lights and looked in the bedroom for her. She wasn't in the bed, or under it, or under the table in the living room. He even looked in the large wardrobe in the entryway. But she was gone. He lay down naked on the floor and fell asleep. The next day he noticed that a few bills were missing from the desk drawer where he usually left his weed money. His passport was also missing. His toothbrush, a stack of CDs. He opened the refrigerator and noticed the curry paste and a little piece of dried up ginger. The next day he felt cheated and preyed upon, and kept going over to the living room window to look for her, but she never showed up. The paper plates looked so pitiful on the dirty sidewalk, the offerings, which apparently were left there for a deity to find between the dog excrement and the overturned bicycles.

One morning, when she had been gone a week, he got more stoned than usual and knocked on the basement door. The fat blonde opened it. "Yeah?" she just said. He stretched his neck to look over her shoulder. But he couldn't see anything moving inside. Then she obviously became tired of waiting.

She slammed the door without saying another word.

THE WOMAN IN THE BAR

I didn't see her come in, but suddenly she's there. She's walking on the polished floor in her heavy boots. She's long-legged. That's the first thing I notice. It's Saturday afternoon and I'm drinking a cup of coffee, watching people; I had an errand to do in the neighborhood, to pick up some dry cleaning, but then I also bought a bouquet of tulips, some tea cake, and a watermelon. My grandchild is visiting tomorrow. I've been walking around the city for a few hours and I'm cold and my legs are tired. It's pleasant just to sit here as it grows darker outside. I've always liked this restaurant. It's large with tall ceilings, white tablecloths, and terrible acoustics. An enormous dining room. People are lingering over late lunch, others are just drinking wine or cocktails, and behind me a couple of children are playing with a small train under the table. The atmosphere is pleasant. I lean back relaxed and enjoy the view of the young woman. Now she's standing at the bar. She's tall and erect, her neck is long and white. It's the end of November. This morning I was thinking about how long it's been since the wall fell. I thought about how quickly time passes. Even though so much has happened. Now the streetlights go on. It looks like it's started to rain.

I like watching people. And this woman is remarkable. She's nearly bald. Her head must've been shaved fairly recently because there's just a fine dark shadow of hair. She drinks carefully out of a small glass, something strong, maybe cognac, or whiskey, I can't tell from here. There's something about her that reminds me of a young animal, perhaps a deer, the same watchful nervousness. She's wearing a suit that's both elegant and a little too large. It's grayish-green, brownish, like mud and dried grass. I have a sudden urge to touch her neck. A flood of images runs through my head: I think about the canvas sacks, about my childhood, about the soldiers' uniforms, and my mother, who, much later, is standing in front of our house outside of Leipzig. It's plastered with thick mortar and has that color so common for East German houses: grayish-green, brownish. My mother is smiling. She's wearing a red dress. My thoughts race. I watch the woman at the bar, this person, this creation, I can't keep my eyes off her. Now I linger on her large meaty hands. I imagine she has a deep sensual voice. The rain is really coming down now, it beats against the large windows, and I notice the doors keep opening. Soaked people step in and wait impatiently to be seated. They shake their umbrellas, brush off their overcoats with their hands, and try to fix their hair. Then she turns halfway. And now I can see her face. It's pale. Her eyes are large and dark, and she's heavily made up with black and brown makeup. I think: dramatic and tasteful. She keeps an eye on the doors, and I can't take my eyes off her face. It's a fantastic face. Full of expression, almost theatrical. She keeps an eye on the doors. Maybe she's waiting for someone. She smokes and runs a hand over the top of her head. She looks at her watch. She empties her glass, throwing her head back to get the last few drops. As she's putting the glass down in front of her, her face lights up in a smile. I turn my head to see whom she's smiling at. He nods and smiles back, raising his hand in an awkward wave. His glasses are steamed up. He walks over, passing close by me, now he's right in front of her. They kiss each other lightly on the cheeks. He says a few words to the waiter who shows them to a table. He shakes his jacket and hangs it over the back of the chair. Suddenly I think about roses. I breathe deeply in through my nose and almost smell the heavy, perfumed scent. I close my eyes and think about all that precedes that scent: the buds of spring, aphids and beetles, heat waves, summer rain. Then, at last, the flowers swelling and unfolding. I don't know why, but I think about roses, about fields full of roses, endless fields of roses, white and red and yellow. When I open my eyes again, they've sat down facing each other and are studying the menu. A moment later they order. She fidgets nervously with her napkin. Her eyes never leave him for a second. I brush some crumbs to the floor. Then he begins to talk, intently and at length.

He does all the talking. She smiles and her eyes move over him like caresses: his face, his hands, his chest. She beams at him. Then suddenly I can't see anything at all. I shake my head. A moment later my sight returns. He talks and talks, leaning forward, leaning back, the mouth going, hands gesticulating, taking off his glasses, putting them on again, then he leaps up and walks over to the stairs to the bathrooms. His corduroy pants divulge a wide ass. Over his shirt he's wearing a leather vest. His glasses flash for a moment, though I can't make out the source of light. He disappears down the stairs. She looks longingly after him. Then she starts tearing the napkin into tiny pieces. A moment later the waiter comes with tea. There are croissants and soup, and an egg as well. She gathers up the bits of paper in her hand and lets them float down over the table. A strange, stiff smile bares her front teeth, which turn out to be separated by a large gap.

The soup is for him. The egg is too, apparently. He eats greedily as she smokes, speaking as he eats; she watches him full of admiration, and the hand she's not smoking with moves closer to his arm, his elbow; without touching him, her hand rests on the tablecloth near the bend of his elbow, as if she were going to grab it, as if her hand were lying in wait. My vision fails again. My eyes burn and sting. I press them hard, turning my knuckles around and around. A moment later, I realize that the couple to the right of me has also noticed them. I'm sure of it. The woman whispers something to her husband.

I see his rounded back under the vest. I see his face in profile, the vague contour of his chin, lost with age. Then she bends forward and kisses him gently on the cheek. He grabs her hand and squeezes it. Their hands encircle each other's, resting quietly on the white tablecloth. I notice the taste of blood. I must've bit my lip, and with my tongue I find the piece of flesh and spit it out into the napkin. It's bleeding surprisingly hard. I notice how dark it's become. The rain's calming down. It's Saturday. Outside the cranes are glowing. I begin to think about something I read somewhere, "Berlin is a wound that no longer bleeds, but a wound that still needs to be scratched." It made me furious, how horribly pathetic that sounds. I shake my head. I unzip my bag. The tea cake has an overwhelming scent of vanilla. I search anxiously for my money and keys. Then I put the bag down on the floor. I raise my empty cup. And now they get up and move across the polished floor, in and out of the tables. The sound of her boots. She's really tall. He's a little shorter and stooped, and it looks to me like he drags one of his feet behind the other. I have a clear view of his left ear. I feel an affection for that ear. He pushes the door open, and she glides by him. I gather my things quickly and place myself in the window. They walk through the red light. He puts his arm around her waist. He squeezes and presses with his hand. They stop under the streetlight and kiss each other. She bends down to make herself shorter so that she can reach his mouth. He squeezes and presses and sticks his hand under her jacket.

It almost looks like she's gnawing on him. She's straightened her back and puts her arms around him, bends her neck, holding her head at an angle. It's a very long kiss. All the while he presses her up against the building. The yellow light from the street lamp falls on parts of their faces. He looks so small. The watermelon is so heavy in the plastic bag. I'm about to drop it. He's opened her jacket, and now he's kissing her neck. For a moment it seems like she's looking me in the eye, and then she throws her head back. She doesn't have a blouse on under her jacket. I get a glimpse of the skin on her stomach. He kisses her breasts. One of my legs is numb. I wiggle the foot but it won't go away. A young man stops and stares at them. She must've noticed because suddenly she closes her jacket. He looks around confused, and again there's that light reflecting off his glasses. She grabs his arm. The young man, who is now walking away, looks back several times over his shoulder. And they take off, arm in arm, Oranienburgerstrasse, cutting over to the S-Bahn, Hackescher Markt. I get a glimpse of her looking at him smiling, and of him putting his head on her shoulder. Then they're gone.

My left leg is asleep, there's a deafening noise around me: the sharp sound of metal and porcelain; high-pitched voices; the music suddenly blasting. It's unpleasant. I have to pee. I turn around and the room seems overwhelmingly large, everywhere people are laughing and shouting and drinking, people crowding the bar, while the doors constantly open and close. The handle of the plastic bag cuts into my hand. There are some spots in my vision, making everything turn so white that I get dizzy, and when I take a step forward, I'm about to fall or sink. Is it roses? Is it paper? My dress rustles and screeches like chalk on a blackboard; a pervasive smell of wet clothes and damp wax paper cuts my nose. Then, suddenly, the boy in the last row who was always throwing small rocks is here; a rock hits and falls on the floor and it startles me. I reach out to stop myself from falling and grab hold of a man's shoulder. His face is blurry. He seems to be saying something to me while I cautiously begin to move slowly toward the stairs to the basement.

I look in the mirror. A face. Speckled, wrinkled. My eyes. A blond woman meets my gaze in the mirror. It stinks in here. My mouth, strangely thin. I splash cold water on my face, my blouse gets wet. Then I drop the watermelon. It rolls out of the bag and splits, revealing a burst of red flesh. The blond woman picks it up and hands it to me. She says something. Everything is blurry: a muddy picture, not of this world. But I can tell that I've received the watermelon. The woman puts her hand on my arm and says something else. I close my eyes and press the melon to my stomach. Fields of roses once more. Then my wedding bouquet as it is now, hanging in the doorway between the living room and the kitchen at home. I see it clearly through the flickering and snot. It's sharp and dry. The image disappears. I think about how it might feel to eat dirt.

Suddenly everything becomes completely clear. I throw the watermelon in the trash and wash my hands. I open my purse and pull out a handkerchief. The scent of the tea cake is nauseating. I throw that out as well. Then I take the clip out of my hair, comb it with my fingers, twist it, and put it up again. It's completely clear that the steel frames he insists on wearing are ugly. He had on a different shirt this morning when I left home. And it's also clear that his hair hanging down like thin tassels from the top of his head means something particular and important about him, about his lifestyle, about his generation. About us. I've never thought about this before. When I at last sit on the toilet and pee, the relief is tremendous. On the way out I throw two coins on the bathroom attendant's saucer. She looks at me with a wry smile. It seems like she's spent far too many years down in the dark, where all that's revealed is a fraction of what there is. I place my yellow tulips before her on the table. Then I walk up and out into the dark.

On my first day in the city I couldn't get enough of walking around. As soon as I had checked into the hotel and set my suitcase down in my room—which turned out to be better than expected, spacious, with a large window overlooking the street, a good bed, thick green carpeting, and a comfortable distance between the bed and the bathroom, which neither smelled nor looked dingy—I decided to stay outdoors for the rest of the day. Elated by the quality of the room, but also by the fine weather, I set out for the city's snaking labyrinth of alleys and narrow passageways and steps. It's no secret that the city is set on a mountain slope, and I enjoyed these ascents and descents, the way the city constantly changed character depending on the height you viewed it from. The city—bathed in sunlight and a dry haze—reminded me in a moving and visceral way how everything depends on who is doing the observing and where you are observing from, and I thought: *This is so incredibly banal, and yet it's so important.*

I bought a red scarf in the bazaar. I looked at the chickens and ducks in small cages awaiting their uncertain fate, most likely to be murdered and roasted, chewed and digested, eventually ending up on the ground or in a porcelain bowl in a completely different state. I drank tea from small decorative glasses. I ate cakes dipped in honey. Then later, at a more refined restaurant, spiced lamb and rice. My hunger was satiated in every way. I climbed the narrow steps, and continued to ascend, while sweat broke out on my back under the thin shirt. I made it all the way up to the enormous mosque that rose in the air in an austere and closed monument, but also as something ethereal and free, and the sight of it made me think of how between the two poles, these two ideals, we seek to unfold our lives. *But I have,* I thought with a joy verging on euphoria, *I have,* saying it slowly to myself, *united these opposites in an action that has given me both control and freedom.* Fascinated to no end by one thing after another: The spicy scent of the flowers and wild herbs growing all over between rocks and asphalt; the men's dark faces and the whites of their eyes that the irises swim in; glimpses of a bare foot or a hand sticking out of a woman's concealing garments; the ancient, thick walls of the buildings. Even the conspicuous poverty moved me because it made me aware of something significant: Life unfolds in different ways, but it's always life; I was in need of such a consolation, partly for personal reasons, because I am not without guilt, but also for the simple reason that those of us who live in extreme wealth fear death and personal decline to an extent that's in sharp contrast to our proven long life span and the multitude of medical advancements and miracles. Such were the thoughts running through my head while I sat, pleasantly exhausted and filled with new impressions, enjoying a drink in a smaller open square in the shadow of a large acacia tree. No breeze stirred. The dull heat of the afternoon vibrated in the air. A couple of children played with marbles. A man was loading vegetables into a pickup. And even though I felt a little like I was being watched since the people higher up could easily see me without me necessarily being able to see them, I felt entirely free of the troubles that I'd been suffering for a long time.

Back at the hotel I took a cool bath late in the evening, carefully washing the wounds and swellings that I had received over the upper part of my body. I changed the bandages covering the deep gash on my right hand, and then I got dressed. I opened the window and inhaled the scents from the dark night, listening to the cicadas and the exotic sounds from the city, and got a sudden craving for a drink.

The bar was nearly empty, a sleepy waiter was reading the paper and drinking a cup of coffee, a middle-aged woman was sipping her whiskey and smoking a thin cigarette. A young man was sitting at a table lost in thought, staring at the large air conditioner on the ceiling that was humming weakly. I ordered dark rum and sat down at the bar. The woman looked over at me and nodded with a smile, lighting a new cigarette. The waiter poured my rum, put on Frank Sinatra, and began polishing the glasses. The rum was good and strong. And I smiled to myself when Sinatra sang "I did it my way" with his soft, unrelenting voice, and I thought, *yes, that's what I'm doing too, that's what I've done, I've taken matters into my own hands, in my own way.* There was something comical about it. The whole wretched business. And whether or not the lightly tanned woman with pretty pinned-up hair wearing an elegant short black silk dress had gotten the impression that I had smiled at her, I can't say for sure, but in any case she struck up a conversation with me. She was English and lived in London, or more precisely, Kensington, and had recently lost her husband. She spoke beautiful English and confided in me that she had traveled here to get a change of scenery and to make a fresh start. I understood, it was the same for me—change of scenery, fresh start—and she smiled, relieved, touching her pearls. I said this is usually why people travel to distant places, and she gave a little nervous laugh and stirred the blue plastic stick around in her glass. Then we sat a while in silence, I finished my drink, but when I got up to go, she grabbed my sleeve and looked at me with clear shiny eyes. "Sometimes my husband was a real bastard to be around. Do you understand? A real bastard." Then she withdrew her hand shyly, and I thanked her for her pleasant company and left. When I lay down in the spacious bed under the white sheet and felt my heavy naked body completely relax, I suddenly laughed. I chuckled and laughed out loud to myself and couldn't stop. "Do you understand? A real bastard."

I spent the whole next day at the hotel. There was a pool in the basement, with an elaborately painted sky on the ceiling so you looked up at white fleecy clouds as you were swimming on your back. There were artificial trees and flowers beautifully arranged in large beds, and the bottom of the pool was decorated with a blue mosaic. It all looked very authentic, even the people lying there as though sunning themselves in lounge chairs around the bar. I stayed a long time in the sauna. I dunked my body down in the cold water right after. Large red splotches spread across my thighs, and my skin received a shock. And that's exactly what I needed. A shock. The wounds on my stomach and chest became soft and turned white from the water and heat. The gash on my hand swelled up. It was certainly good for the healing process, and I sighed with contentment: soon the traces on my body would disappear like dew in sunshine.

I had a good lunch in the restaurant and drank half a bottle of wine. As I was wiping my mouth, I felt a light touch on my shoulder. It was the Englishwoman. Now wearing a blue suit. I invited her to sit down, and she did so without any hesitation. We ordered coffee. In the daylight I could see her face clearly, the thin lips, greenish eyes, lightly freckled skin with more wrinkles than I had noticed in the dim evening light. She talked about her daughters, one was a nurse and the other a teacher. She showed me a photo of her grandchild, a stout, fair-skinned four-year-old boy. "And you," she asked, "do you have any family?" "A sister, a brother, and a sea of nieces and nephews," I answered. She let out a short sparkling laugh. "That sounds delightful," she said, "a sea of children!" And she threw her arms open wide as if she were about to embrace this sea of children and laughed again. A gold tooth glimmered deep inside her mouth. Then she asked me if I wanted to join her sightseeing in the city, but I declined, saying that I unfortunately had some work to do. Without hiding her disappointment, she asked what kind of work I did, and I got the idea to say that I was writing an article that I needed to finish by the evening. "Oh," she said, "You're a journalist?" And I got the idea to say that I was a writer and I was writing a series of travel articles on the Middle East and Turkey. Her eyes opened wide with enthusiasm. "How exciting!" I smiled and did my best to look both flattered and modest. She gathered up her things, wished me luck with my work, and left. But when she reached the door, she turned and came back. "I just realized, I never introduced myself," she said. "My name is Ellen Parker." She put out her thin hand and let it rest for a moment in mine, light as a baby bird and cool as the white sheets on my bed. I walked back to my room. The wine had made me drowsy and I slept like a rock for two hours.

The next morning I woke up early and felt uneasy. It was clear that I couldn't stay any longer in this city. And since I had no desire to meet Ellen Parker again, I left the hotel without having breakfast and wandered around the city for a few hours. Even though it was warm, the air was fresh at that time of the day, and I watched people one after another slowly opening their stalls and stores, I watched the sun slide higher in the sky while the children walked to school with their books in their arms, and the traffic became louder, the heat more intense. The city's awakening made my brain work faster and more directed, the feelings that had driven me out of bed and onto the street receded, making it possible to get an overview of my situation. On the one hand, I still wanted to rest and store up energy for the long journey home, on the other hand, Ellen Parker was a problem. I had tempted fate with my lies and had a feeling that she would seek me out again and try to force herself on me. I feared that she sensed I was keeping a secret, and that she, without really realizing it, had the urge to reveal it. I feared she had a *sense* about me.

I sat down on a low wall and looked out over the valley. I thought things over. And decided to make a compromise: I would stay, but only one more day, and I would avoid contact with the Englishwoman.

In the afternoon I returned to the hotel. I asked the young man at the front desk to reserve a plane ticket for me, and went upstairs to my room. The window was half open, the maid had made my bed and brought fresh flowers. As I was changing my clothes, I noticed a white envelope on the dark green carpet. Someone must've pushed it under the door. The letter was from Ellen Parker, of course it was. Her handwriting was large and looping. It was a polite invitation to dinner at an "exclusive restaurant" not far from the mosque. I sighed and crumpled up the letter. I sat down on the bed, suddenly too tired to put on my clothes. I lay down and closed my eyes. I began running my hands over my body, a strong desire surged up in me. I lay on my side for a long time watching the thin curtain billowing a bit even though there wasn't any breeze to speak of. Ellen Parker had green eyes and attractive hands. Strange how this could move me so easily. Maybe it was simply because I hadn't talked to anyone for more than two minutes in such a long time. I dozed. And woke with a start. The telephone was ringing. My first reaction was to let it ring, but then I remembered the receptionist, maybe there was some information about my ticket, so I answered it. And it was Ellen Parker. "Oh," she said, "I hope I didn't wake you." She wanted to know if I would accept her invitation. I said I couldn't spare the time to have dinner unfortunately, the work was giving me problems and it was taking longer than expected, and she said that I would need to eat in any case, but we could meet at the hotel restaurant instead to save me the trouble of walking up to the mosque. How did that sound? Eight o'clock? I said that I was thinking about having some food sent up to my room, and she said that that sounded cozy, and would I like to have some company, she would leave as soon as we were finished eating because she understood quite well that I had work to do, of course she understood that I had important things to take care of, and she would in no way disturb me, but it is after all rather boring to eat alone. And that was that. Even worse than I imagined it would be. Ellen Parker, not just in a neutral place, but here—in my room, next to my bed. I immediately put away all my personal belongings. I looked at myself in the mirror. Turning my face so that I could almost see my profile. Then I filled the bathtub. And just as I got into the warm water, the phone rang again. It was the receptionist. The flights were all booked. I asked him to reserve a seat on the next available flight. In four days. Sitting on the edge of a chair, naked and dripping wet, I tried to accept the fact that I wouldn't be leaving for four days. It wasn't until I began shivering that I got up and went back to my bath.

I considered walking out. I considered moving to another hotel. But it was likely that I would run into Ellen Parker somewhere, sometime, and the prospect of facing an awkward, and no doubt dramatic situation like that seemed too great. And, in my confusion, I had already reserved the room for four more days when I talked to the receptionist on the phone. The room was expensive. I was depressed and angry. If I had previously found the situation comical, it now seemed grotesque, and I wasn't laughing.

Ellen Parker stood in my doorway in an olive-green dress, smiling. She'd brought a bottle of Chablis. She kissed both my cheeks lightly. Her gold bracelets jingled. I made a show of stashing a stack of papers in the drawer. They were all blank. Then I ordered lentil soup and warm sandwiches from room service. I tried to open the bottle of wine but the cork was too tight. Ellen Parker took the bottle from me, and without any trouble, screwed the bottle opener into the cork and pulled it out. I was stunned. Where did she get all her strength? She smiled and poured the wine into our glasses. We looked at each other and made a toast. "To your work. May it be a success!" she said. We sipped the wine. It was cold and refreshing, like filling the mouth with summer flowers, and suddenly I felt a longing for home. Then a boy came with our food. She sat in the armchair, I, at the desk. We struggled to eat neatly despite the fact that we were both in awkward positions. Finally, I gave up trying to eat my soup with a spoon and instead lifted the bowl up to my mouth to drink. She glanced at me with shining eyes, and then started to crack up. "Oh my god, oh my god!" she kept saying. I also started to laugh even though I really didn't feel like it. And a moment later, when she slurped her soup, I slapped my thigh and threw my head back in wild laughter, while a deep darkness spread through me. I had completely lost control. And I heard myself shriek with laughter when Ellen Parker spilled soup on her olive-green dress and then drooled from her open mouth when a new convulsion of laughter rolled through her. She put her hand on my knee and, gasping, tried to speak, but it wasn't possible. She tried to wipe the spot with her napkin, but that also got us going again like delirious children, and soon I was crawling around on the floor trying to keep from laughing, my stomach muscles cramped up and tears streamed down my face. Ellen Parker lay face down on the bed shrieking hysterically and kicking her legs up and down. One shoe was off. At least ten minutes passed before we got hold of ourselves enough to control this fit of laughter; with red cheeks and messy hair, we tried to straighten out our clothes. Ellen Parker picked her shoe up from the floor and turned her back to me and put it on. I got up and filled two glasses with water from the bathroom. We drank greedily and, almost at the same time, set the glasses down in front of us. I sat in the armchair, and she, on the bed. Ellen Parker lowered her eyes. "You'll have to excuse me," she said almost whispering. "I don't know what came over me."

I grabbed her arm. "There's absolutely no need to apologize," I said, leaning toward her with a spontaneous tenderness for her that almost made me cry. "I started it." Then she looked up at me and smiled. Now she looked almost transparent. "It's been a long time since I laughed like that. Thank you." In silence we ate our sandwiches, which had become cold. She poured more wine into our glasses. "You see, it hasn't been easy since my husband's death. But I'm beginning to understand that it also wasn't easy when he was alive. I feel ashamed to say it, but it's almost a relief to be alone." She lit one of her thin cigarettes and leaned an elbow on the bed. She was nearly lying down. "I know exactly what you mean," I said, "exactly. It's nothing to be ashamed of." Then she suddenly got up, stubbed out her cigarette, and said that she should go so that I could work and that she had already kept me from it for too long. I took her hand, it was warm and a little moist. I watched her walk down the hallway. Her bracelets jingled. She turned and waved. There was a strong scent of her cigarette and perfume in the room. I thought about opening the window but didn't. She had pulled the cork out of the bottle like a man and succumbed to laughter like a little girl. I paced back and forth, emptied her wine glass, and felt like an animal in a cage.

The following days flew by. I no longer remember the order in which things happened. But one night I forced my way into Ellen Parker's room. I took off all my clothes. She stood paralyzed in the middle of the room staring at me in the dim light. "I thought…it can't be true," she stammered. "I was certain that you…were a man." She gasped, holding her pearls. Then she put her hand on my chest. Gently, she caressed my wounds. "I almost believed it myself," I whispered. Then I pushed her down on the bed. She trembled. We lay there with each other a long time.

From then on we enjoyed the city together. We climbed up and down the narrow streets, taking in the view from different angles. I gave her the red scarf I'd bought in the bazaar. She gave me one of her bangles. Once she asked me about my injuries. I didn't respond. Another time, about my work. I said that I'd finished it long ago. Ellen Parker was a shining light for me. The morning I left we exchanged tear-filled good-byes.

She ran after the taxi as I drove away. I haven't seen her since. But a year later I went to London and wandered through Kensington, imagining her life there. Her daughters and the grandson. Charity work, perhaps. Another wealthy husband, perhaps. When you've taken the life of another person, you see those who are still living in a different way. I never get tired of looking around.

MOSQUITO BITE

March

On Thursday, he'd been out on the town all night. He was drunk. A woman with shiny high-heeled boots came on to him, and he ended up going home with her. He can't remember if it came to anything more than some fooling around and sleeping. He simply can't recall—*did* they have sex or not—it's impossible to remember. When he woke up the first thing he heard was a strange scratching sound. Scratching and scraping and then a peeping sound as well. Something living was puttering around alarmingly near, and he froze. He opened his eyes. But it wasn't until he came up on his elbows that he realized where the sound was coming from. at least forty hamsters were darting around in their cages stacked in a high tower, one of them rested its front paws on the chicken wire and was staring him right in the eye. He shivered. Then he heard a flush in the bathroom and the woman, who looked clearly older than he, staggered across the room, white as a sheet, drying her mouth with the back of her hand; she had likely been throwing up. She fell on the bed groaning and pulled the blanket over her. It smelled stale and sour. He hurried to get up and dressed. On his way out he noticed that the apartment was a mess, completely filthy. When he got out to the street, he had no idea where he was at first, but then it became clear to him that he was on the outskirts of Copenhagen. He felt fine actually. He bought a cup of coffee and began to walk toward the center of town. His sister was arriving home from London that day and they'd made plans to go straight from the airport to the summerhouse. It was drizzling. Quiet rain. Nice on the skin. He looked at his watch and picked up his pace. His thoughts lapped gently in his head: It was good that he was in excellent shape, that's probably why he didn't have a hangover. It was good that he'd gotten lucky. It was good that it was raining, and good that he was so horny, that meant at least that he had something good to look forward to. He crossed the Town Hall Square. A flock of greedy pigeons picking at rice on the steps flew up in a fright when he walked through them. Fifteen minutes later he let himself into his apartment in Christianshavn. Twenty minutes later he had showered and dressed. He boiled two eggs and packed his overnight bag. Then he squeezed a couple of oranges and warmed some milk for more coffee. He only had time to skim through the news-paper and eat his fill before he drove to the airport.

He noticed right away that Charlotte had bought new per-fume on her trip. He couldn't figure out if the dominant scent was jasmine or orange blossoms. She looked good, fit. They hugged and he kissed her on the cheek. She laughed at his bloodshot eyes, and he told her he'd been out with the guys from his office and they had forced him to do shots. She stroked his cheek. He sped up. It looked like it was going to be nice weather. They talked about how he needed to cut the grass, and about their mutual friends who were coming for dinner and would stay overnight. They decided to make cur-ried lamb with the meat they had in the freezer.

She had bought new sheets in London. Sateen. And three pairs of shoes. The show had gone well for her. He turned up the soft, ambient music, she stopped talking and relaxed. Suddenly he remembered that the woman had been wearing a garter belt. Now he remembered that he had stripped her panties off her. It was going to be a wonderful Easter. Their brother and his children might come on Sunday. Then he'll hide Easter eggs in the garden and be fun and avuncular. He smiled and looked for his sunglasses. The sky was cloudless and the spring light was so bright it almost blinded him.

That evening they got cozy on the futon couch with their blankets. She had made cardamom tea. He watched the news on three different stations, she read magazines. They gossiped about their mother and laughed. He felt tired and warm.

The next morning he went for a run on the beach. There was nearly no wind. The sand was wet from the rain during the night. He enjoyed the cold salt air, he felt strong and at ease and decided to sprint the final leg; lyme grass and sand as far as the eye could see.

When he got back, Charlotte was setting out lunch on the patio. He did his exercises on a yoga mat in the hallway, stretching at the wall bar. They ate. He put more logs in the fireplace. She hummed in the kitchen while kneading dough. He rested. Then he went to cut the grass. The neighbor looked over the fence and greeted them. Charlotte waved from the kitchen; now she had a towel on her head and her face was covered with a white facial mask. She looked like a clown. When he was finished with the lawn he drank a cold beer. It's useless to rake up clippings when they're wet. Then they started to make dinner, and at six o'clock Stine and Jakob arrived with Emily in a bassinet. They both knew Jakob from elementary school, and he had also gone to high school with him. Charlotte had hung small gold and silver eggs from a bouquet of birch branches. The meal was well prepared and the wine, delicious. The women talked about Charlotte's boutique and how difficult it was to find a good au pair. He told Jakob that he had to hire two casting directors for a new TV show on homes of the rich and famous. Jakob asked if people weren't tired of such programs but he said that they'd found a whole new spin on the subject. At around midnight, when Stine and Jakob retired to the guest wing, Charlotte also went to bed. He relaxed in the living room with a glass of cognac and noticed the light from the kitchen pouring out the open door onto the wall bar in the entryway, illuminating it so that it shone, red and warm. And suddenly he saw Maja, his ex-girlfriend, leaning against it, one evening when she had been lying seductively on the bed, but he had wanted to take her standing. And so she held onto the wall bar with both hands, and it was only because his thigh muscles were so strong that they could do it in that position. The thought had crossed his mind right before he came, and was maybe even part of the pleasure. He laughed at the thought, emptied his glass, and got up to do the dishes.

The next morning was the first time he noticed the mosquito bite. It itched on his left buttock. He must have gotten it when he was cutting the grass. They waved good-bye to Stine and Jakob and went for a long walk. Charlotte said that it was so wonderful to take time off. She really needed it, moving the shop to a better and larger location had really taken its toll on her. She looked sweet in her green rain jacket, like when they were children. He could smell himself. They went through the pine forest, where it was dark and slate gray, the dampness rose from the ground, Charlotte looked at him and said something, but her eyes had changed to dark holes, she looked like a skeleton, he thought, stopping to take a piss.

In the evening he noticed there was an opening in the mosquito bite. He had obviously scratched it. It was Saturday. They watched a movie and drank the rest of the wine. Charlotte fell asleep during it, snoring lightly with her mouth open. Suddenly he remembered that the woman with the shiny boots had rolled a joint in bed. But he still couldn't remember if they'd had sex. He shook his head, irritated.

But the bite was really tender and swollen when he showered on Sunday morning. He got Charlotte to look at it. She washed it with some rubbing alcohol and he winced and she said he was a baby and slapped his behind; he pretended to faint, then sprang up and howled like a wild animal and she hunted him down through the house; they laughed. A horn sounded in the driveway loud and long, then the door opened and Pete, their brother, sauntered into the living room, ruddy-cheeked and loud. The children had already run out to the yard to climb the trees. He went outside to bring them in for lunch, one in each arm, both of them squirming and squealing with delight.

They had herring and schnapps. Charlotte made an effort to be friendly to the children. But they were out of control, running from the table constantly, peeling the painted eggs, knocking over a beer, crawling up on his lap and pulling at his beard. He thought it was pleasant to have a little warm kid sitting on his lap, but Charlotte was clearly not amused. As she used to say, she didn't like children, and now she looked obviously put off. In contrast, Peter didn't seem to notice the commotion. He talked about the divorce, getting himself all worked up, until finally he was forced to signal to him that children with their big ears were nearby. Charlotte got up and helped them into their jackets and they ran right out and started throwing the newly cut grass at each other. As Peter was talking, he realized that he'd never hid Easter eggs. If he left right now, maybe he'd still be able to buy some. But he didn't feel like it, and it really didn't matter now. Peter poured some more schnapps. He'd always been so damned impulsive. He was never in control of anything. And now his wife had had enough. Peter's eyes looked wild, he pushed his chair back, stretched his legs, and hit the table with his fist, "It's fucking bullshit that she'll only let me see the children on the *weekends!*" And then at last it came out that she'd already met someone else. To top it all off, it was an old geezer with a shitload of money, as he put it. Charlotte seemed like she was going to give him a lecture, then suddenly she looked bored. She went into the kitchen to make coffee. The mosquito bite was fucking painful now. He felt around and noticed a large bump. It had evidently not helped to clean it. Peter calmed down, then began to cry. Charlotte came in the door rolling her eyes and shaking her head as she was drying a green glass bowl. He promised that he would try to help Peter find a better apartment. Maybe there was someone in the office who knew of something. He'd make a few calls. Peter blew his nose in the napkin. Then the children came bursting in completely covered in wet grass and mud.

In the middle of the night he woke up feeling miserable. His buttock was throbbing. He woke up Charlotte, who reluctantly got out of bed and turned on the light. She could see that there was an infection and the bump was hard and red. "It looks like it's turning into a boil," she said, yawning. Then he made her get a pin, hold it in the flame of the gas burner, and prick a hole in it. She pressed out the puss, shouting, "Yuck, disgusting!" He clenched his jaw. She told him he could get some aspirin in the bathroom, and then she turned off the light. The next day they cleaned and locked up the house. He carried their bags out to the car and closed the trunk. A blackbird belted its song from the tall birch tree near the driveway, and he caught sight of a whole bunch of snowdrops shining white on the wet black ground. An unusual feeling of loss, emptiness, sadness—he couldn't put his finger on it—welled up in him. But there was also joy. The blackbird, the flowers, and the sun, which was already low in the gray sky, hidden behind passing clouds. Then Charlotte came out and began to talk about how he should hire a man to lay the paving stones she had ordered for him from Italy. "You'll enjoy the house more if you have a proper terrace," she said. When he got home there was a message from their mother. She really wanted to see them on Easter, but maybe next week? He erased the message and put on the Red Hot Chili Peppers, turning it up and opening the door to the roof terrace. The gold cupola atop the tower of the Church of Our Savior shone dimly in the dusk light. His buttock throbbed. *It'll pass*, he said to himself, *it's nothing, it'll soon pass.* Then he took a shower, got dressed, and went down to the local bar and got a couple of pints of draught beer, and his spirits quickly lifted talking to the bartender and some guys from a rival production company, and then he saw Heidi come in the door, loaded, accompanied by a fat girlfriend, and this suited him because the last time they were together was wonderful. So he got up from his rivals' table and shouted, "Hey gorgeous!" and she threw her arms around his neck. He could smell the liquor on her breath, *an angel must've sent you.*

Later they stumbled into his apartment, took off their clothes and threw them on the floor. He turned his back to her to turn on the light and she bent over to wrestle her feet out of her tights, then she got up and caught sight of his butt. Terrified, she let out a scream. He turned toward her. "Turn around again. What the hell is that?" He had almost forgotten about it. She walked over to him. "Turn around," he just stood there shushing her, grabbing her and kissing her throat, and she searched with her hand for what she had seen and then froze and pulled back, "Have you gotten the bubonic plague? No, stop it! *Stop* it! There's no fucking way I'm having sex with you when you've got that…what is it, it must hurt like hell!" He persisted. "It's nothing, come on, Heidi." But Heidi wanted to wash her hands. And she wanted to go home. She forgot her tights. He was pissed. He wanted to screw her so badly, he really needed it.

A few days later, while he was in a meeting with a Swedish colleague and his partner Stig, it began to hurt so badly that he couldn't concentrate. He squirmed uneasily around in his chair. As the day went on the entire cheek swelled up more and more. In the evening he had a fever. He called Charlotte. He lay on his stomach freezing, and Charlotte said, "Christ, you should see yourself, you look like a baboon." She sighed deeply and carefully laid her hand on his lower back. She said it looked like there was a whole bunch of small boils around the large one. She called their uncle, who was a doctor, and he laughed, joking that he always knew he was a bit of a pain in the ass. Their uncle called the doctor from the emergency room, and when the doctor came at 10:30 and took one look at him, he asked why in the world he hadn't gone to his own doctor a long time ago, and sent him to the emergency room. The boils needed to be cut away.

And they were. He threw up into a paper bag. The pain was beyond words. Afterwards the nurse put a compress of gauze on it and told him that a home-care nurse would come and change the bandage once he got home. He thought about old people needing to be washed and their diapers changed. They kept him in the hospital for two days, and gave him a round of antibiotics. He lay on his side in the bed, tried to work, dozed, and watched TV. The fever subsided a bit. He insisted on going home. His mother picked him up and he lay in the backseat, quiet and drained. "You just need to concentrate on getting better, honey," his mother said. "Will you please stop it. I'm not SICK," he said. "It's just a mosquito bite for Christ's sake."

He called Stig and told him that he'd be out the next couple of days. He took his pills. Every morning the nurse came, a meticulous, straight-backed woman who looked like she'd been very beautiful once; she pulled the bloody gauze off, washed out the wound, and put on a new bandage. But then the fever went up. He called her Gorgeous. She smiled and shook her head shyly as she took his temperature. He had no appetite, only a constant headache, and in time, pain in his sinuses. After he'd been home eight days, the nurse arranged to have an ambulance bring him back to the hospital for new blood tests. It turned out that he had contracted a staph infection while he was in the hospital. More antibiotics. Then home again. Charlotte came over with soup and red wine. But in the middle of the night he woke up because he couldn't breathe. He roused Charlotte, who had fallen asleep on the couch in the living room with all her clothes on as she usually did. She got up, dazed, and turned on the light. Then she screamed, clapping her hand over her mouth. He was swollen up beyond recognition, his torso, his throat, his face—red, thick, and deformed. Charlotte ran to the phone to call an ambulance, whimpering, hysterical. He tried to get up, but she yelled, "Don't move! Don't move!" In the ambulance they immediately gave him an injection. They took his vitals. Then put on the sirens. He could hardly see out of his eyes. They raced him down the long corridors, and at last they arrived, a sea of anxious faces gathered around him, becoming one gray, blurry mass.

It was the penicillin. He was allergic to it. The doctor explained to him, "You had a violent allergic reaction. You got here just in time. We have your sister to thank for wasting no time in making that call!" The doctor smiled and patted his shoulder. But the next morning the results of the new blood test arrived, showing that it was clearly a case of resistant bacteria. He yelled at the staff and refused to wear the ridiculous robe, not to mention the underwear. He didn't like the food, he didn't like the smell, everything was disgusting. This place makes you sick, he raged. His room had small low windows. The hospital was built at a time when they all economized on glass. He couldn't stop thinking about this as he lay there. Every time he looked over at the small peepholes and out to the world, he thought about it. *1973. Maybe '75. The oil crisis. All they could think about was saving money on expensive materials like glass.* It drove him crazy.

April

He was sick. They sent him home. He came back. Very sick. New medicine. Home. Gorgeous let herself in and rustled about somewhere near him. Her cool hand against his warm skin. Back to the hospital. More tests, a biopsy, blood tests, urine tests. Pus began flowing from his ears, his eyes and nose were clogged and sticky with green gook, he felt nauseous all the time, and eventually got diarrhea, later, blood in the diarrhea. He watched the transparent tube where the sulfa drug went through in drips to his vein at the back of his hand three times a day. His uncle called and demanded to talk to the head doctor. This can't be true. There must be something you can do. There wasn't. "Yes, there is," said Charlotte. "We can hope and pray that you get better." He had no strength to either hope or pray. By this time, he felt like a slab of meat rapidly decaying. But also: *It's not true*. Denial. Aggression. Later, panic attacks and difficulty breathing. He changed from one medicine to another. And to different types of medicine. The infection spread. He was moved to his own room. He was delirious. Peter visited and took one look at him and cracked up laughing. And he laughed with him, as best as he could, almost grateful for his brother's laughter, his completely ordinary reaction, "Holy shit, you look awful!" But it got worse. And it went quickly. No strength left to sit up, push the call button, scratch his leg, hold a glass of water.

The doctor repeated what was already known, "Unfortunately the bacteria are in theory multi-resistant," and he sat down on the edge of the bed. "We've decided to move you to the General Hospital. I've already talked with them and they can take you as early as this evening." The doctor leaned forward and said confidentially, "I have to be honest with you. We can only hope for the best."

June

Isn't it summer? He tries to wave hello. Charlotte smiles, but she doesn't know how to comfort him. She calls their mother even though that's the last thing he needs. Their mother is shocked by how much weight he's lost. She brings roast chicken and mashed potatoes and feeds him with a teaspoon. He throws it all up. He wants her to go. That anxious old mourner's mug. She cries into the mashed potatoes. He feels guilty. He closes his eyes and pretends to sleep. He opens them a little, and now she's eating what's left of the food with the teaspoon right from the Tupperware thingy. Later, he actually does fall asleep. And there's a waterfall tumbling over rocks and a sound that's about to burst his head open. *Isn't it summer now?* Then he's on his knees on the floor in the little bathroom throwing up. He's in the infectious disease ward at the General Hospital. "This time you're staying," said the doctor. "Your immune system is burned out, you might say, and we'll do all we can, but no promises." He has fungus growing in his mouth, in his intestines, on his hands. He's lost almost all of his hair, and, in three months, he's lost fifty-five pounds. When Charlotte calls Stig, thinking he's asleep, he overhears her saying, "When I was here yesterday, two nurses helped him to the bathroom, they wanted to give him a bath. I'm standing in the doorway and he vomits this thin green fluid into the sink. Then I see diarrhea running down one of his thighs, and he passes out. Oh my god, Stig, I thought he'd fucking died, just like that, collapsed. But there was a pulse. They asked me to get help, and then three people lifted him up and carried him back to bed. It's so humiliating. You can smell him from far away. You've got to visit him."

He thinks about what he's touched. Did he touch the toilet? Did he touch the chair? Did he lean on the chair on his way to the sink? Did he touch some bacteria, perhaps some bacteria found its way into his body? He doesn't want Charlotte to get too close to him. He keeps asking her to wash her hands. She stops coming by so often, she has to take care of her shop, get ready for the sale, it's a busy time with the big summer sale. And, as she says, crying hysterically, "I've got to live my own life, don't I? I've got to look out for myself." It's something she's realized, she says, after thinking long and hard about it for almost three months. She gets loaded at Stine and Jakob's garden party. She sits on the lap of a young man and sings.

He doesn't notice that she stays away for long periods of time. There are visions and shadows and faces that come close and then disappear. There's nausea like a snarling dog pressing its wet fur against the inside of his esophagus. There's a constant whistling in the pipes or maybe from his body. They have grafted skin from his thigh to his buttock. He doesn't remember. Charlotte says, "They've done an excellent job," but he doesn't believe her. His mother talks to him with the same consoling, loving voice she had when he was a child. She keeps talking to him until he calms down, and he *does* calm down, listening to her voice, as if it came from above, as if it were flowing into the room like liquid or gas.

Finally, Stig comes to see him. He pushes the door open, and puts his hand to his mouth in shock, as if he's seen a ghost. Then he backs out. The door closes quietly. A little later he comes into the room and sits on the edge of a chair. He has a big bouquet of dark purple flowers on his lap. He whispers, "What have they done to you?" The bedsores hurt. He doesn't have the *strength*, for conversing, for holding up his head so that he can look at Stig. And Stig says, almost angrily, "For Christ's sake man, how long have we known each other? A long time. Right?" He looks down, "I never thought that..." And Stig puts the flowers on the nightstand, lays his hand on the blanket, and squeezes it, swallowing hard. *Get those flowers out of here.* He can't think about anything else. Stig had touched them and then the blanket, *for God's sake, don't touch me.* Stig gives him a pleading look. But he closes his eyes, and when he opens them again, Stig's gone. At night he asks for a mirror. The nurse holds it in front of him: His cheeks are sunken, his skin hangs in large gray folds, his eyes are yellow, he looks like someone about to die. A corpse. He turns his head and looks at his inflamed ears. He'd already seen his hollowed out ribs and sunken stomach. His arms and legs that have transformed into bones covered with skin. He has felt the top of his head. But the face. He wants to scream, he has no strength. "Sleep well." The nurse is standing in the doorway and has turned off the light. She leaves. And he cries.

July

To see your own face. Now he's tormented by violent panic attacks, they give him medicine for this as well, and it helps: he sleeps better and more, it's as though his thoughts were padded with wool, no longer knocking hard against each other; he receives intravenous feeding, oxygen, morphine, he calls for a bed pan, he asks for music, and they bring it, he listens to the Red Hot Chili Peppers, and the edge of pain is taken off.

Charlotte sits in the window seat swinging her legs. Smiling, she hesitates to tell him that she's now seeing Stig, and that they're in fact in a relationship. "Isn't that great?" He grumbles. "Aren't you going to congratulate me?" *You've betrayed me.* She, in the sunlight with the blue sky behind her, his rage reduced to sniveling, *no strength.* Charlotte says, "It's funny, isn't it? If you weren't here, I would never have noticed him, NEVER!" She giggles. "He's not exactly a hunk, is he?" And then, dreamily, "But we understand each other, I've talked a lot lately—about you—and your illness, you know, that's how we got to know each other. Are you sleeping?" She hops down and comes closer. He swipes at her with his limp hand. She looks troubled, "I thought you'd be happy." He tries to smile. All is lost, he's given everything he has, he can't do any more. And the days run together with the light nights, suddenly he comes down with pneumonia, high fever, he has a nightmare about the hamster cages, dreaming that he's trapped with the scratching animals; everything is going downhill, they can't *stabilize* him.

One day the head doctor sits on the edge of his bed and says that he has to give it to him straight: it'd be a good idea if his family from Jutland, his sisters and father, visit him now. The doctor keeps looking him straight in the eye with a serious and compassionate expression, but he fails to understand even this hint. "Why in the world should your so-called *father* come now? What business does he have here? He's never once bothered to send you so much as flowers!" The mother is beside herself, her voice rises. Charlotte gives her a beseeching look. The mother sniffles, squeezing his hand. He pinches her as hard as he can, and she pulls away frightened; he asks Charlotte to wash his hands with soap and water. "And rubbing alcohol! Put gloves on. Put rubber gloves on before you wash me." He shakes his contaminated hand in the air. "For Christ's sake, go get a washcloth, NOW!"

Then his father and half-sisters arrive. And his mother and Peter, Peter, pale and shy this time. They say good-bye. Yes, that's what they're doing. They sit at his deathbed holding back their tears. Then Charlotte says, "That's enough. He's tired out." They back out of the room with dark eyes. She pulls the blanket up around him. "Don't die. You're not going to die. Just you wait and see." And he thinks she smiles. But she winces when she gets out into the hallway. Because she knows she's losing him, but she doesn't know if it's her fault. She runs a little, desperate to get out into the cool summer night.

When they detect meningitis, he's given a new kind of medicine that's hard on the kidneys. He turns yellow. They're afraid his muscle mass will be permanently damaged. They say that the medicine is working. But the blood tests still show an infection. Then it looks like it's beginning to have an effect. And he, he has no suspicion about the threat of death. He has no intention of dying. He puts on the headphones: "Give it away, give it away, give it away now..." The bass pumps, he rocks his head from side to side on the pillow, and looks out at the evening turning blue, the moon half hidden behind the drifting clouds. *Did I have sex with her or not?* And then suddenly he remembers. He didn't. He couldn't get it up! He smiles to himself, it's so funny, imagine that, he *couldn't* do it, he was healthy and strong, but he couldn't get his dick to cooperate, and now he also remembers that they shared a joint afterwards, when he'd given up, and she had been so shit-faced that her eyes rolled around in their sockets, then she fell asleep with her head in his lap; that's how it was.

March

He opens the main door and *falls* onto the street. It's raining. He can't get up. He tries to get up on all fours, but his body refuses. He simply lies flat on his stomach on the dirty wet sidewalk. There are a few people at the bus stop watching. Then, at last, an older couple comes over to him. They could be his grandparents. He takes their hands and with great difficulty, he hoists himself up. A couple of teenagers hide their laughter. A young woman turns her back. He thanks the old people, and leans against the wall of the building with one hand. Then he starts to move up the street with small steps. As usual, he feels pins and needles in his feet. They say there's chronic nerve damage. Charlotte is furious at him. In a way, that makes it easier. He'd rather not be bothered. His clothes hang on him. He lives on pork chops with gravy, but he only gets fat around the waist, it doesn't distribute evenly, so he still has toothpick arms and toothpick legs, but he doesn't have the energy to use the exercise bike, he *can't be bothered*; it takes him at least ten minutes to crawl up to his apartment on the third floor; he smokes a lot of dope, *that* helps, he sleeps better, it dulls the anxiety—his fears, simply. There's so much he understands now, which he can't bear to understand: he is terrified to die, he's afraid of being sick—*cancer, heart attack, a boil on the ass*—there's so much he's come to realize, the underlying frailty, how close he was to kicking the bucket, and then the fact that his life has broken into a thousand small discordant pieces, it can never again be as it was, he's not the same person anymore, no pride, no joy, no recognition: THIS IS ME, but whatever he is, he doesn't know, he has no idea how he'll *move on with his life*, as Charlotte put it, when she also told him *it's sink or swim* and slammed the door, he could hear her shouting something else on her way down the stairs.

He smokes, turns up the music. And suddenly starts laughing, loud and heartfelt: Shit, when he was at Peter's and his new girlfriend's wedding last week, he threw up and got such a pain in his stomach that his mother had to drive him home; shit, there wasn't anything fucking wrong with him, it was just stress, all those people, no, nothing was wrong, it was just that he was suffering from an imaginary sickness, that's so fucking funny and so to hell with everything, he's sold the summer house, he will sell his share in the company to Stig, he's staying here, ordering pork chops from the take-out place across the street—they're so kind to deliver it to him—dragging himself down the stairs to buy dope, and then: ah, sweet sleep, sweet refreshing rest, thank the Lord; he sits down and cracks opens his long-anticipated beer, suddenly feeling like a newborn with everything to look forward to.